SAVING GRACE

HER FATED MATE
BOOK 4

EMMY LOU HAYES

Published by Blushing Books
An Imprint of
ABCD Graphics and Design, Inc.
A Virginia Corporation
977 Seminole Trail #233
Charlottesville, VA 22901

Saving Grace
Her Fated Mate Book 4
By Emmy Lou Hayes

eBook ISBN: 978-1-63954-563-6
Print ISBN: 978-1-63954-631-2

PROLOGUE

1722

KERRY, IRELAND

TORIN LOOKED DOWN AT BETH AS SHE LAY IN HIS ARMS, HER CHEST heaved heavy breaths, her breasts pressing against the corset of her dress. He bent and kissed the tops of them.

"We will leave, together. We can cross the sea to Scotland," he whispered in her ear. "I do not care what my family has to say. I wish to be with you and you alone."

"I love you, Torin." Beth kissed him quickly. She couldn't believe how incredible the time they had spent together had been since she came to the O'Gannigan Keep with Faith.

She was a mere maid in the arms of an incredible man, and he loved her for who she was.

"I've my things packed and ready," she told him as they both shifted on the bed and rose to their feet.

"Aye, we must make haste." He held his hand out to her, and she placed hers into his.

The couple crept down the servant's stairwell and out the

back door of the Keep. Seamus was waiting for them. Torin had trusted his brother in this when he had no trust in any other. Seamus came to him and told him that his father had ordered him to kill Beth, to keep their secret. Together they came up with the plan for the two of them to escape. To save Beth's life.

Through the night the three of them made their way over the knolls of the O'Gannigan lands, crossed through town and were nearly to the edge of the Keep's boundaries when they heard it. The howl of a wolf shattered the night. Beth screamed, fear streaking through her.

Seamus and Torin both jerked their heads up looking for the wolf they knew was coming. They scanned the trees. Torin was the first to see him, their father emerged from the darkness. He shifted and ran towards him, Seamus following suit did the same. The two wolves collided with the largest of them as he rushed toward Beth, standing frozen beneath the moonlight.

Growls and snarls ripped through the air. Torin was thrown to the ground more than once. Continuing to find the strength he needed to protect her he rose again and challenged his father. As he rushed him once more the older wolf dodged his attack and his claws ripped into his brother's side. Seamus yelped. Falling to the ground, before Torin's eyes he shifted back to his human form.

The reality of the damage he had caused, of what he had done took him over. He whined and approached Seamus. His nose pressed to Seamus's chest. Declan took advantage of the distraction, sneaking up behind the slip of a woman who stood shaking with fear watching the scene unfold before her.

"Torin!" Beth's scream pulled him back to the present.

Jerking his head up from Seamus he looked on in fear as his father lunged for Beth.

"Go!" Seamus yelled at him. He knew he was already healing. Knew he didn't need his brother's help. Beth did.

Torin put every ounce of strength he had into running as fast as he could toward Beth and Declan. A scream cut through the air, and his heart shattered in his chest as he watched Declan take Beth down. Her body hit the ground with a sickening thud. He reached her seconds after it had happened. Declan retreated from his position over Beth's body.

Torin skidded to a halt next to her, looking down into her eyes as the last of her life faded from them. Tossing his head back, he howled. Then he shifted, scooping her into his arms and holding her tightly to his chest.

"Beth, please," he begged. Tears slipped down his cheeks. "Please, look at me. Beth!" He called to her again and again. Her head lolled to the side, the blood stains spreading over the front of her dress. "No!" he screamed, his throat raw with it. "No, please. Beth, I love you. We are going to leave this place together. Come on wake up." A hand settled onto his shoulder, and he jerked. Turning to look at Seamus standing behind him.

"Torin," Seamus bent beside him, looking down at the woman in his brother's arms, "she's gone."

"I'll kill him!" Both brother's looked around for their father as Torin spoke.

He was gone, coward that he was he couldn't even face them or what he had done. He slunk away with his tail between his legs as soon as the deed was done.

Torin collapsed forward over Beth's body, he wept into her neck for hours. As time passed and the sun began to rise, Seamus shifted on the ground next to him.

"Let me help you," Seamus pled with his brother. "We need to get out of the open."

Torin nodded, rising to his feet with Beth cradled in his arms. They carried her into the woods a way. When he laid her down on a bed of wildflowers they found a proper place, shifting, they used their paws to dig the grave. As Torin settled her into it gently, a bundle of flowers on her chest he kissed her cheek one final time. Seamus helped him to cover her with dirt and they stood side by side as they looked down at the unmarked grave.

"She deserved so much more than this. This is my fault. I should have been able to control myself, to keep our secret from her. She is dead because of me," he wept into his hands as he spoke.

Seamus sighed, he knew this was not the truth, this was not Torin's fault. They both knew who was actually to blame.

"We need to return to the Keep. Everyone will be waking," Seamus patted his brother on the back and turned.

"I'm not coming," Torin called to Seamus. "I can't go back. I'll kill him." His words were filled with so much hatred. His heart in pieces.

Seamus heard the truth of it in his brother's words. He nodded and watched as Torin shifted and took off into the trees. When he disappeared over the horizon he was met with a single howl. It broke his heart for his brother, to hear the pain in it. He knew if he saw him again it would not be soon.

CHAPTER
ONE

1822

KERRY, IRELAND

TORIN'S HOWL OF PAIN RIPPED THROUGH THE NIGHT. THIS WAS THE first time he had returned home, returned to this place in one hundred years. He imagined he could still smell her here. Could still feel Beth's blood soaking the earth. His chest hurt, the pain he felt was insurmountable. A whimper slipped from his lips as he saw a figure moving in the wood line. The silhouette of a wolf emerged from the darkness.

Seamus looked into his brother's eyes, the anger, nay, hatred he saw there tore him in two. His deep scars ached with the memory of the last night they stood together in this clearing. The sound of the woman's screams filling the night air around them as their father snuffed out her life. This place haunting them both, the ghosts of the past meeting them here in this moment.

Torin shifted his legs beneath him, rising to his feet as his brother approached. Contemplating his next move, he had remained in this form, wolf through and through for so long he knew not how to even begin to return to the world of man.

Unsure what drove him back here after all this time and caught off guard by Seamus's presence in this place, on this night no less. He didn't believe in coincidence, if they were both here it was time. They needed to speak. He needed to return and face his demons. Each shifted, standing as men in the clearing. The silence around them palpable.

"Torin," Seamus started, "Brother…" His voice cracked.

"Aye?" It was all Torin had to offer. One hundred years without words, with his own thoughts. The wilderness crept into him, he at last had become one with it.

"You've returned? At last?" Seamus needed to know if he was truly coming home. If this was the night that he had been waiting for.

Torin simply nodded. He was ready, willing. He would go with Seamus to the Keep. He would face his father and what he had done to him. But he vowed that night so long ago, and he still felt it to be true in his heart, he would never forget. If forgiveness was possible, he would open his heart to the possibility, in time. Alas, he knew he was still not ready to take that step.

Return he must, a wolf can only survive without his pack for so long and the pain he felt at being parted from his brothers had been mounting with each passing day. Taking a step toward Seamus as his brother opened his arms to him, he fell forward into his embrace.

At last, he was home.

2024

.

DUBLIN, IRELAND

. . .

GRACE SAT AT HER DESK IN THE TRINITY LIBRARY COMBING through the books that lay open before her. She had waited long enough. It had been centuries. She would take matters into her own hands.

The previous year she had met Cassidy, and the two had become close over the past twelve months. Knowing she could ask her friend for help in this she planned out her trip to Kerry, to the O'Gannigan lands, and at last to her destination. The dolmen that was still standing on the Keep would provide her with enough magic to cast the spell she had written.

Being half Fae she had the magic in her veins and she had used it in her lifetime more often than not. This feat, however, would prove difficult, she needed the magic in the land to lend her the strength her half-blood powers did not provide.

St. Valentine's Day was a week away, it was the perfect time to invoke her spell. She smiled down at the piece of notebook paper in her hand, the words she had scrawled across it in the old tongue.

"This is going to work," she squealed.

The last thing she needed to do for her plan to work was call Cassidy. She needed her friend's help. She knew the O'Gannigan clan was territorial, knew they were ancient, Seamus and she had once been close. When she needed his help nearly a century ago, he had been more than willing to stand by her side against the Fae who claimed he was her father. She had always wondered about Shay and his family. What secrets they had and the truth of what they were. Immortal members of the magical community, no doubt. But they guarded their secrets and their land closely. It wasn't until Seamus had introduced her to Cassidy that she felt she would have the in she needed to use their land for her gain.

Pulling her phone from her purse she quickly typed out the text to Cassidy. Then sat, waiting, praying to the Gods that the time had finally come, and she would meet her fate. Love had evaded her, human men were fun for a time, but alas they aged, and she did not. They would not endure the passing of time the same way she did. Fae men turned their noses up at her half-blood. Refusing to lower themselves to her level.

Her life had been a lonely one. When her mother passed, and she was left to fend for herself, she began dreaming of finding the one. A man she could love with her whole heart and live the rest of her immortal life with by his side. Now, she decided to take matters into her own hands.

She would conjure him, the perfect man, her perfect mate, fate would bring him to her in the end. She simply needed to give it a nudge.

THE BUZZING OF HER PHONE DREW HER ATTENTION FROM HER thoughts, and she hurried to look at the message from Cassidy.

Cassidy: *Oh my gosh, I would love it if you came to visit for Valentine's Day! We can have a girl's weekend!*

Guilt nagged at her heart, she needed to tell her friend the truth. She didn't want to use her in this way. She truly did want to spend time with Cassidy, and her sisters-in-law who she had heard so much about each time Cassidy came to Dublin for research needed to write one article or another.

Grace resolved to tell Cassidy the truth once she arrived in Kerry. She would tell her all about her plan and maybe even having someone to help would be an added benefit.

But she couldn't keep this from her friend. At last, she had a girlfriend who would be with her through the test of time. Another immortal to share things with, while she craved love and desired a man in her life, losing her bond with her friend would not be worth it.

Quickly she texted Cassidy back, rereading it she knew it sounded cryptic. Knowing Cassidy, though, that would intrigue her more. Grace smiled as she hit send on the message and waited. Cassidy's name flashed on the screen and Grace smiled as she hit the button on her phone connecting the call.

"Oh my gosh, am I actually going to get to witness you using some of your Fae magic? Like for real!" Cassidy rushed out the words, then squealed.

"Yes, calm down." Grace had promised her she would show her some magic. But only if she promised not to make a story about it for the newspaper she worked for.

"I can't... This is so exciting! What are we doing? It's on Valentines Day? Oh my god! Is it a love spell?" Grace rolled her eyes as Cassidy gushed on the other end of the phone.

"I'll tell you everything when I get there. What day should I come?" She looked over at the calendar hanging next to her desk.

"Come Friday, we will have a girl's night. Do your spell Saturday, then you can head home Sunday. Sound like a plan? I doubt Shay has anything planned for us."

Grace winced, she knew she would be keeping her newlywed friend from her husband on Valentines Day. "You don't think Shay will mind?" In truth, she was more worried that Shay and his family would be upset at having a stranger in the Keep for the whole weekend.

"Pfft!" Cassidy responded. "I don't think he even knows it is Valentine's Day."

"No, I mean, do you think he will mind having me there in the Keep?" Cassidy was silent at her question.

She knew whatever the O'Gannigan secrets were that Cassidy was bound to keep them. It is why she never pushed her for answers. Being a Fae herself she understood keeping one's truth private. Six months ago, Cassidy had blown Grace's own secret wide open, it was a long time coming, hiding who she was from an investigative journalist she spent so much time with that it was bound to happen.

"I'll ask Shay. But I think it's fine. Plan on Friday!" Cassidy squealed again. "You're gonna love the girls!"

Excitement filled Grace, she knew she was going to have a good weekend, regardless of the outcome. Cassidy would see to it.

"I love you, Cassidy. I'll see you next Friday." Her smile spread over her face. Everything was coming together.

KERRY, *Ireland*

ONE WEEK LATER

GRACE STOOD ON THE FRONT STEPS OF THE O'GANNIGAN KEEP kicking the toe of her shoe against the steps. At last, the door swung open, and Cassidy rushed out to hug her. As soon as her friend wrapped her in her arms, she melted against her. The stress of what she had been planning had overwhelmed her this past week and all the tension that had built up in her body relaxed away as she let Cassidy hug her.

"You're here! Come in!" Cassidy grabbed her hand and pulled her over the threshold into the great hall of the Keep.

As Grace looked around at the murals that covered the walls and the ceiling her eyes went wide. Shay had been right to keep her at arm's length, so many answers came to her now that she was here in this place. The truth at last revealed to her.

"Grace," Seamus's voice reached her across the hall as she saw her old friend approaching. She had no doubt the men who followed close behind him were his brothers. They all looked so similar. Their features were ancient.

"Shay," she said and sent him a small nervous wave. Not wanting her face to give away what she now suspected about the clan, nay the pack. "Thank you for having me. This place is incredible."

"It is, may we speak?" Cassidy turned and raised an eyebrow at her husband, frustration filling her that he was coming off so rude to their guest.

"Aye," Grace nodded. "I had little doubt that this conversation would be due."

Seamus turned to Cassidy, he knew Grace would see the truth of it all now that she was here, and he needed to make sure they could trust her. Needed his father to be aware, his stomach turned at the memories of the things they had done in the past to keep their secrets.

"Cass, why don't you go and find Faith and Olivia. I think they're in the nursery. I just need to speak with Grace for a moment." Pulling her to his side, he planted a kiss on his wife's cheek and ignored the questioning look she gave him.

"Grace?" Holding his hand out to her, Seamus motioned for the door at the end of the hall.

Grace tensed but followed him, she knew this was a mistake. She could have insisted to Cassidy that she only come for the day and stay in town.

As Seamus, Cormac, Brody and Grace piled into Declan's study Grace turned. The eyes of what she now knew to be four werewolves trained on her face made her nervous.

"Let's not beat around the bush," the older man behind the desk in the study they just entered cleared his throat and said. "Grace?" He nodded in her direction.

"Sir?" She tensed under his gaze. The look in his eyes told her that this man was capable of things she couldn't imagine.

"I'm Declan. You know my son Seamus, these two are Cormac and Brody. I'm not going to pretend that I don't feel it rolling off you. The Fae magic. Nor will I pretend that you don't suspect the truth about us." As Declan spoke Seamus took his place next to Grace, Brody and Cormac each took a seat on the couch against the wall.

All eyes were on her. "Werewolves," she whispered the word low under her breath.

"Aye, Seamus has managed to keep it from you for the years you have known one another. However, it seems Cassidy has managed to let the cat out of the bag."

"No, no. She didn't. I just..." she paused, thinking through her words carefully before she went on. "I knew you were immortal, magical, I had my suspicions. The murals." She pointed to the door they entered through, back to the hall. "That was what gave it away. I won't speak a word of it." Rushing out the last part. "I know the importance of keeping one's secrets."

"Aye, I suspect you do," Declan stared into her eyes. "Then that's settled," he said at last.

The tension in the room was starting to dissipate. Seamus and Grace both visibly relaxed at clearly being dismissed by Declan. As the Alpha of the O'Gannigan pack sat behind his desk he thought through the ramifications of someone knowing the truth of them and how his youngest son would respond. He would need to speak to Torin.

Seamus turned to Grace, sending her a small smile as they both headed from the study back to the great hall.

"Well, that went well," Grace said dryly. "I'm sorry to have caused trouble for you. I should find Cassidy."

As if she had been summoned by the mention of her name Cassidy appeared at the end of the hall, a redhead and a blonde that Grace suspected were Faith and Olivia were in tow. The blonde held a small bundle in her arms.

"Grace! Ready to head to town and get our girls weekend started?" Cassidy called to her. Seamus rolled his eyes at his wife as she approached.

"Stay out of trouble, please. It is all I ask of you four for the weekend," Seamus growled low in Cassidy's ear.

Cassidy stepped back, an obvious flush spreading over her face made Grace giggle. The connection between her two friends ran so deeply that it made her ache. She yearned to have the same for herself. Soon, she thought to herself. One more day and she would have her perfect mate.

THE AFTERNOON SPENT IN TOWN WITH CASSIDY, FAITH, AND OLVIA proved to be exactly what Grace needed. As they sat around the table in the booth at the pub following their time at the spa the ladies chatted carelessly about their lives. Grace felt at home with them, she felt as if she were building bonds that would last her lifetime and it filled her with joy.

"So, what are all the romantic plans for Valentine's Day tomorrow?" Cassidy asked the women surrounding her. Knowing that the O'Gannigan men were romantics at heart she had little doubt that Faith and Olivia would have big plans for the next night. She chewed on her lower lip. Wanting to share with them the plans that she and Grace had, but knew Grace wanted to keep it just between them.

She had asked her earlier in the day to tell her all that was to follow the next day, but Grace insisted they wait until they were alone. Grace still needed to bring up the dolmen to Cassidy and her nerves as the topic was brought up were getting to her.

"Brody and I are going into Dublin! Dinner, I think. You know when you've had a few hundred Valentine's Days together it's hard to come up with fresh ideas." Faith shrugged, Grace and Cassidy both looked in her direction. They couldn't fathom being with a man so long.

"Same," Olivia sighed, "plus the wee one is still on the tit and I doubt we will be able to be gone for long. Speaking of," she looked down at her watch, "I need to get back. I feel like I'm going to burst. I'm a damn cow these days."

The other three women laughed, Faith scooted out from the booth to allow Olivia to stand. "I'll come back with you. Let these two gal pals have some time without us old ladies," Faith told them.

Grace was happy to have spent the time with them, but thanked the stars that she would get to speak to Cassidy alone once they were gone. As they said their goodbyes and sat back down in the booth Cassidy and Grace both felt a thrill of excitement flow through them.

"Tell me now!" Cassidy burst out at last.

"I'm going to cast a love spell to bring forth my true mate. I need you to take me to the dolmen on the O'Gannigan lands," Grace said. She had at last let her friend in on the plan she had cooked up.

"If it doesn't work, I have someone I can introduce you to. After all, there is one O'Gannigan left to be claimed." Cassidy winked at Grace, but in her heart, she knew it was only a tease. Torin had been through so much that Cassidy doubted he would ever love again.

"That's sweet, but it's going to work. At midnight tonight we need to be in the center of the standing stones. Can you pull it off?" Grace eyed her.

"Of course," Cassidy scoffed, confident in her ability to manipulate her husband and sneak her friend from the Keep.

"You're sure it won't be an issue with Shay? I don't want to get you in trouble, if you show me where it is this evening I can go alone." Grace didn't mind being on her own for the spell, for a moment she even considered it, wondering if it would be a better idea. "Maybe, that's what we should do," she told Cassidy.

Cassidy nodded, she wanted to see the Fae magic, but she also knew it would be hard to slip away from Seamus in the middle of the night. Not wanting to blow Grace's chances she decided to go with the latter idea but pouted over it.

"Okay, let's go. I'll show you where it is," Cassidy sighed.

"Thank you. I promise, I'll show you magic this weekend. Just not this spell," Grace said and smiled at her friend as they stood and headed home from the pub.

"So, TELL ME HOW IT WORKS?" CASSIDY ASKED AS THE TWO WOMEN walked over the knolls toward the dolmen. Grace could make out the tops of the stones in the distance as they approached.

It hadn't been a long walk from the castle and Grace had taken careful note of the trees, stones, and paths they had followed.

"I cast the spell, and it will summon my mate. Simple as that. There really isn't much to tell." Grace looked over at Cassidy who was in awe of her friend's capabilities. Cassidy knew she had become immortal and was married to a werewolf all in the past year, but to actually have her own magic would be incredible. She was rather jealous if she admitted it to herself.

"That's so fucking awesome! Will you help me write a story about it? It would make for a great column. A Fae who cast a spell for her true love, Dan would eat that up!" Cassidy squealed.

Grace raised an eyebrow and looked over at her. "I thought we had talked about this and decided no stories about the Fae?"

"I know, but they keep asking me. It is such a legend in Ireland and since I moved here, and they agreed to let me work remotely, I kind of have to do as they ask. I figure it is better to have you help me with a Fae story than do it on my own," Cassidy said and shrugged.

"I'll think about it. I have a friend we can ask, too. She might be willing to help." Grace stopped talking as the circle of standing stones came into full view. She was the one in awe now.

Being so close to the ancient Fae mound that she knew was the place where the Druids had chosen to erect their dolmen she could feel the magic buzzing in the earth beneath her feet. It would be incredible to be able to tap into it.

"There it is," Cassidy pointed.

"It is amazing! I can feel the magic already!" Grace wanted to take off running for the circle of stones. She wanted to stand in the center of it and summon the magic to her. That is exactly what she would do tonight.

"Do we have time for you to show me something now?" Cassidy wiggled her eyebrows at Grace, hoping she would convince her to give her a view of magic. Anything would please her. A slight of hand party trick, honestly, would be enough.

"I don't think we have time. Aren't we supposed to be having dinner with the family?" Grace asked, stalling. She didn't want to pull from the well of magic here to entertain Cassidy. She wanted to harness it for her spell and the purpose she was here for. "Plus, you'll get an even bigger kick out of my friend when you interview us for your article. She is full Fae and can show you so much more than I can." Grace knew it was dirty, she felt a twinge of guilt. The truth was though, they did have dinner plans and she didn't want to waste any of her energy now with party tricks when she had such a massive spell to perform tonight.

"Ugg, you're right. We do need to get back for dinner." Cassidy sighed. "Did I tell you about my first dinner with Gwen? I almost killed Shay that night."

Grace turned and followed Cassidy back down the hill toward the Keep as she listened to her tell the story of the night she met her mother-in-law, and the horrid dinner she had to sit through knowing that all of the werewolves at the table could smell what she and Seamus had done together on the side of the road.

"I have to say, I'm extremely relieved that you finally know. Keeping it a secret from you for this past year has been killing me," Cassidy said and pulled Grace to a stop. "When Shay told me that is what you all were talking about when you got here, I was shocked to be honest because of what happened with Torin and—" Cassidy stopped herself, realizing she was saying too much.

"What? What happened?" Grace's curiosity was piqued.

"Nothing, I said too much. It isn't my story to tell, and I shouldn't gossip. I'm just happy that you are in on my biggest secret now," Cassidy said and pulled Grace into a hug.

The two women made it back to the Keep just in time for dinner to be set out on the table. All throughout the meal Grace made small talk with Gwen and Cassidy. Listening to the other's plans for their romantic evenings together the next night. But her nerves were getting the better of her. She bounced her knees beneath the table, trying to calm herself. It was only a few more hours before she would be attempting to cast her spell.

Cassidy walked Grace to the guest room on the second floor of the Keep after everyone else had finished dinner and they had spent some time with Seamus in the great hall chatting. Standing outside of the bedroom door Cassidy hugged Grace.

"Good luck," she whispered in her ear, "call me if you need anything. I can't wait to hear how it went in the morning." Cassidy kissed Grace's cheek and headed down the hall back to the apartment she shared with Seamus.

Grace closed the bedroom door behind her. Looking around at the old-fashioned room, it was obvious the family hadn't updated this room in decades, centuries even. But she figured they didn't often have guests, since they were hiding such a massive secret about themselves.

Her bag was sitting on the edge of the bed, she went to it

and pulled out a fresh set of clothes and her toiletries. Checking the time on her phone, she had enough time to shower and get herself ready to meet the man of her dreams. Besides, she needed to kill some time to allow the others to all be asleep so she could sneak out.

As she stood under the water of the shower, she hoped it would ease some of the tension in her neck and shoulders. She was on edge and eager to have this night over and done with. The minutes ticked by as she dried her hair, did her make-up and got dressed. At last, she sat on the edge of the bed, checking the time again, she saw she still had two more hours until midnight. It wouldn't take her that long to get to the dolmen and she didn't know how she would kill the time.

Pulling the spell and the things she needed from her bookbag she packed them into the tote bag she planned to take with her. Then, second guessing herself, she pulled the spell back out of the tote bag and read over it. Two, three, four times she read the spell. She had confidence it would work but wasn't sure of some of the wording. Chewing on her lower lip she wondered if she should change it now, but decided against it. She was committed.

TORIN STOOD IN THE HALLWAY OUTSIDE OF THE GUEST BEDROOM. He didn't know what had drawn him here, this wasn't the first time he had felt the pull to this place, and it ate at him. He had spent the dinner standing just out of sight at the top of the stairs trying to catch a glimpse of Cassidy and Seamus's friend.

His father had tried to track him down earlier in the night, and he knew why. Knew what he was going to tell him. It sent him into a rage. This girl had come into their home and discovered their secrets, and she was allowed to live. He thought about that as he had paced up and down this hall for the past hour, pausing periodically outside of the bedroom door.

Seamus had filled him in on everything while the women were in town. He understood that she was part Fae, she had secrets of her own. The rationale that it was no different than the Fae or the other wolves knowing their secret was one that hung heavy on his heart right now. She wasn't Beth, she wasn't an innocent human. She was an immortal, so she was allowed to know. It seemed unjust to him.

Perhaps that is what kept drawing him here to her, the idea that she knew what they were and was being allowed to live.

GRACE CREPT from the Keep as silently as she could. Knowing that werewolves possess superhuman abilities she hoped she wouldn't be discovered. Seamus was being thoroughly distracted by Cassidy, and the other brothers seemed to be just as enthralled with their wives after dinner. But the mysterious Torin had still yet to show his face and she had no chance of getting out of the castle if she came across Declan.

The full moon overhead gave her more than enough light to make her way over the knolls that covered the countryside as she headed for the dolmen that Cassidy had shown her earlier this evening. When Grace arrived, she crossed to the stone that was being used as a table in the center of the standing stones and began to pull her supplies from her bag.

Torin watched from the wood line. He saw her sneak from the Keep and, though he had been avoiding her all day, something drew him to this woman. He could smell the Fae on her and decided that was all he was feeling, that mixed with his emotions over her knowing the truth.

As she pulled items from the bag slung over her shoulder, he watched her closely. Curiosity over what she was doing here in the dolmen and so obviously preparing to perform magic of some sort, had his eyes locked on her. When she began to speak the space around her filled with orbs of light. The magic she invoked pulled up from the earth beneath her feet.

Suddenly the draw he felt to her tugged at him and he stepped forward from the place where he crouched in the trees. His feet moving of their own will, he had no control over his body. Her long curls cascaded down her back as she tossed her head back, face turned up to the full moon. A howl ripped from his throat as he too jerked his head back and glared at the moon above them.

He needed to go to her. Needed to shift and take her in his arms, claim her, he knew in that moment she was his mate. Knew suddenly, in his heart, what she was doing. The day had nearly slipped his mind. It was midnight on St. Valentine's Day and his mate was casting a spell to call him to her. Just as he made the decision to shift and go to her he heard it, a roar ripped through the night.

Grace's head turned and she saw the wolf standing near the trees, but she knew the roar hadn't come from him. She continued to speak the words of the spell she had written so carefully. A second roar followed this time by a growl broke through the night and the crashing of a beast in the trees moved closer to her.

Torin and Grace looked on as a massive bear burst out of the woods into the clearing. Torin, having control of his body again took another step toward the woman. The bear running head long in her direction. He knew in that instant he wouldn't be able to beat the beast to Grace. Her scream filled the night as it collided with her, and she fell backward onto the ground.

Torin dashed toward them, just as he reached the edge of the circle of standing stones he froze. He thought for a moment his mind was playing tricks on him. Instead of finding Grace beneath the body of a beast that no longer existed in this time or place, he saw a man holding her in his arms.

Confusion filled him, his mate had summoned another. The truth of it was right here before his eyes, but it made no sense. Perhaps he had been wrong, perhaps she was not his mate after all and what he had felt moments before was the pull of her Fae magic.

Grace lay on the ground, fear coursing through her as she looked up into the eyes of the massive bear. When its body began to shift in front of her eyes, she gasped.

"Ach, lass. I meant not to frighten you." Grace's body shook as he wrapped his arms around her.

Pulling her into his lap as he sat back on his heels, he looked down into the face of the woman who had summoned him. A wicked thought came into his mind as he felt her body tremble beneath him, a memory from centuries before when he had taken another woman, one he was forced to take in his other form.

As he felt the warmth of her skin against his own, he realized what he had become, realized what she had managed to do. He was holding her in his arms. He was free. No longer banished to live in the bowels of the earth and free to roam, not as a dark shadow forced to control the wildlife, but as a man. He tossed his head back and laughed, Grace looked on thinking he was magnificent, an incredibly gorgeous man, laughing as he held her in his arms.

"I," she gasped, "it worked." Grace's hand reached up and brushed the side of his face.

Turning his cheek into the palm of the woman who dared touch him, he smiled and said, "Mmm, at last."

Grace could feel his girth hardening beneath her behind as she shifted in his lap and blushed. Her blush only deepened as he looked down into her eyes, lifted his hand and placed it on her cheek. Leaning down toward her their lips met and magic exploded around them. Grace moaned into his mouth as he claimed her. When he pulled back from her, she was breathless, her breasts heaving as she gasped for air.

"Grace," she murmured out her name. "I'm Grace."

"Mmm, my sweet saving grace, I am Rowan."

A twig snapped behind the couple and Rowan jerked his head to the side, his eyes glowing a deep red in the night, Grace unable to see his face, craned her neck toward the sound. Rowan saw it, the silhouette of a wolf backing into the trees. His chest rumbled with a growl. He would bide his time with the wolves, end them one by one, but now he had other needs he must sate.

Torin's heart raced as he looked on, something about the man he heard call himself Rowan seemed so oddly familiar. The red eyes, the beast he had been when he emerged from the woods. The truth of it nagged at the back of his mind. He crept away under the cover of darkness, unsure of what he had just witnessed. But determined to get to the bottom of it.

Grace let out a soft whisper, "Rowan?" His name sounded so sweet on her lips to them both.

"Grace?" He turned back to her. He would let the wolf go for now. He moved, grinding her over his cock.

"Mmm," she moaned, tilting her head back and exposing the soft white flesh of her neck.

Licking his lips, Rowan bent and kissed her collar bone. She tasted incredible, felt glorious to hold in his arms. At last, he would have what he for so many centuries had craved. Hands roamed over Grace's body, down over her belly to the hem of her shirt, then up over her chilled skin. The wind kissed her exposed breasts as he pulled her shirt off over her head, she cared little about the winter breeze, the heat growing inside her from this man's touch was driving her mad.

Rowan looked down at Grace with a hunger in his eyes that

made her ache deep inside. Her pussy tensed as he trailed his fingers in a circle around her nipple.

"Sweet Grace, I have waited centuries for your siren call. Do not make me wait a moment longer." She nodded at his words, granting him the permission he requested.

She had called him here to her through time and space, not knowing from where, and caring so little of the repercussions. She knew at last she would not be alone. Rowan stood, taking her with him in his arms. As he set her on the low stone table in the center of the standing stones his hands slid down her sides to the waistband of her jeans.

Fingers working over the button and zippers he quickly pulled them down over her hips as she braced herself on her hands and lifted her ass for him. Sitting naked on the cold stone she began to shiver in the winter night's air as Rowan's eyes trailed down over her body.

"Amazing," he said and licked his lips.

Grace blushed at the hungry look that filled his eyes. Her own traveled down over his bare chest to his groin. His massive cock bobbed as he stepped toward her.

Fisting himself in his hand, he got lost in the feeling of it. The feeling of him. Having a body of his own. When he stroked himself as he stepped forward again, he tossed his head back and roared. The sound more animal than man. Grace giggled. This bear of a man who had been summoned from the wilderness for her was something to see.

She wiggled on the stone. "Rowan," she said, then looked into his eyes as they came back to meet hers, her fingers sliding down over her hip to her pussy.

"Mine," he growled low under his breath at her and she stopped her movement. "Mine," he told her again as he replaced her hand with his own.

"Fuck," Grace cried out as he circled her clit.

Positioning himself at her entrance, he pushed forward into

her and she moaned. "Rowan, yes. Please," she said and wrapped her legs around his hips pulling him deeper into her.

"FUCK! YOU FEEL INCREDIBLE WRAPPED AROUND MY COCK," HE murmured in her ear.

Rowan had taken women in his other form, but it did not compare to what he felt now. The heat of her velvety walls wrapped around him made him arch his back and buck inside her.

"Mine," he growled again, Grace felt the reverberations of it in her chest as he pressed his body to hers.

"Yes, Rowan," she cried out. Tensing down around him as his fingers, between their bodies continued their motion over her clit.

"Master," he looked into her eyes, his flickered red for the briefest of moments.

Grace nodded. "Yes, Master." She heard herself say the word, her movements feeling almost robotic for the briefest of moments.

Rowan grinned. This new body was proving useful, his powers growing inside him. He would have her, he would guide, control, and use her. The Fae scent on her skin told him she would prove useful. Now, his mind settled on one thought, breeding her. Marking her as his own. Claiming her body, then her mind, and at last her soul.

Taking hold of her hips he lifted her off the stone and set her on her feet. "Turn around," he whispered in her ear as he slipped from her heat.

Grace nodded, turning and bending over the stone, she swayed her hips from side to side. Then feeling Rowan's hands on her hips as he drove forward into her, she cried out.

"Master!" He had been right, this was right, she needed to address him as such. It felt right in her soul.

Rowan fucked her in earnest then, hard and fast, he needed to fulfill the craving so many years in the darkness had caused inside him. Wrapping a hand around the back of her neck he pinned her to the stone beneath them.

His other hand came down over her ass, smacking her hard. She gasped, pushing herself back onto him, craving more of the roughness.

"Mmm, good. You want it rough and hard, my sweet Grace?" Rowan asked her as he smacked her ass again and again. Pounding forward into her.

She began to buck beneath him, the feeling of her orgasm spreading up from her toes, through her body straight to her core. She tensed down around him tightly. Rowan could feel her body milking his cock.

"Mine!" he called into the night again as he filled her with his cum.

When he stepped back Grace's body quaked from her orgasm, and he watched his cum drip from her. The sight was incredible, it filled him with pride at having at last taken a woman in this way.

"Rowan," Grace called to him as she stood. Shivering from the cold.

"Get dressed, we must leave this place. I know where we can go." Rowan's words made her heart sink as Cassidy came to the forefront of her mind.

Her friend would wake in the morning looking for her, but she couldn't leave him. She couldn't walk away from this man, her mate she had summoned, and return to the Keep. She hadn't thought that through. She hadn't expected it to work, if she was at all honest with herself.

"Come," Rowan held his hand out to her, shifting and falling to all fours beside her.

He was again in his bear form. She quickly dressed, gathered her things and climbed onto his back. Rowan took off into the night.

CHAPTER
FOUR

TORIN HADN'T GONE FAR. He gave her the privacy she deserved. But as he waited in the woods, he heard them coming near. The sight of the bear with Grace on his back came into view, making their way through the trees towards him. He ducked down behind a log and waited for them to pass. He needed to figure out what had happened, what this magic was that called forth the bear shifter, Rowan. Who was this man who claimed his woman in the night?

Seamus was his first thought. His brother might have more information he did not. As he watched Grace go, the same pull he had felt drawing him to her previously, called out to him again. Tilting his head to the side he wondered at it, could it be real? After all this time mourning the loss of his Beth could his true fated mate be here, on his lands, in the arms of another man?

The idea of it tore his wounds open once more. He had possibly found her at last. After he'd returned to his home he'd wondered if he would ever find her. A part of him still believed that his fated mate had been Beth and she had been lost to him the night his father snuffed her out. Turning in the opposite direction from the pair he headed to the Keep, to his brother. He needed answers and that is where he would seek them.

"Seamus?" Torin called to his brother from the bedroom door. He hated to wake him, hated to intrude, but he couldn't wait for morning.

"Torin?" Seamus rolled in the bed, Cassidy in his arms. Confusion at seeing his brother in his apartment in the middle of the night quickly turning to concern. "I'm coming, hang on." Seamus jumped up and found a pair of pants, pulling them on quickly and meeting Torin in his living room. "What's wrong?"

"It's Grace," Torin said and rubbed his hand over his jaw as he sat on the couch.

"Grace?" Seamus immediately thought that perhaps his father had changed his mind.

"She went to the dolmen. I followed her."

Realizing by Torin's words that his first instinct was wrong, his confusion grew and he sat next to his brother.

"She is Fae?" Torin asked.

Seamus nodded. "Yes, half-Fae. I helped her with a full Fae who claimed to be her father, nearly a century ago now. The dolmen?"

"Aye, she performed a spell. Summoned a bear shifter. He calls himself Rowan." Torin let this information sink in before going on, "They left together. But there is more, this man, this Rowan. His eyes glowed eerie red in the darkness, he seemed to have power over her. Have you heard of such things?"

Seamus shook his head, but thought through his brother's words. "A bear shifter? Power over women? It almost sounds like the Dorcha. But that lifeform was banished three centuries ago, and it held power over the wilderness. Are ye' sure?"

"Aye, positive. There is more." Torin sighed.

"What more?" Seamus grew uneasy.

"I believe she might be my mate. Grace," Torin clarified.

"We will get to the bottom of this." Seamus said and listened, hearing Cassidy before she entered the room.

"The bottom of what?" she asked and yawned as she emerged from the hall.

"Grace is gone," it was Torin who spoke up first.

"Gone?" Cassidy crossed to them. "Her spell," she murmured the last part under her breath. There was no point, the brothers both turned inquisitive eyes to her.

"You knew?" Seamus stood and crossed to his wife. "What do you know, Cass?"

Cassidy felt shame fill her at keeping things from him. She hadn't wanted to lie, but an omission was still a lie in a way. Sighing, she made her way to the kitchen to the coffee pot and started it brewing.

"She had a love spell. She said she needed me to show her the way to the dolmen so she could perform it at midnight." Her words were flat, and she winced at the look in Torin's eyes.

"A love spell, that explains it. The draw. It confirms what I suspected as well." He turned to Seamus.

"She is your mate?" Seamus asked him softly.

"Grace is Torin's mate?" Cassidy practically screamed the words.

"Gods in heaven, woman, you'll wake the entire Keep. Keep your voice down," Seamus scolded her.

"Sorry." She winced at her error in judgement. "Grace is your mate? The spell summoned you?" Excitement coursed through her, she and Grace would be sisters, but her heart dropped the next moment. "What do you mean she is gone?"

"Aye, the spell also summoned Rowan. She has left the Keep with him." Torin shifted uncomfortably on the couch. "But if she was in fact using a love spell to summon her mate, then that proves my suspicion to be true. I had been drawn to her all day. Then in the circle of stones the magic drew me in so strongly. I cannot deny it."

"Who is Rowan?" Cassidy asked, her confusion growing by the minute.

"A bear shifter," Seamus said and turned to Torin. "We need to see Da' and wake the others."

"Bear shifters are a thing?" Cassidy bounced on the balls of her feet, feeling a story piecing itself together in her mind.

"Nay, they are not. We do not know what the truth of it is." Torin stood. "I'll get Cormac and Brody. Meet me upstairs."

Seamus nodded, turning back to Cassidy. "Stay here." She raised an eyebrow at him.

"Over my dead body. I'm calling Grace!" Cassidy ran from the room to get her cellphone.

"Cass," Seamus followed her into the bedroom, "stay here!" He commanded her this time. The unease he felt over what this creature was had him worried for her safety.

"Yes, Sir," she replied and sat on the edge of the bed. "But I'm still calling Grace."

"Fine!" Seamus turned and left the room.

Torin entered his father's study with Cormac and Brody close behind him. Declan and Seamus were already there.

"What is the meaning of dragging me from my bed in the wee hours of the morning?" Declan demanded from Torin.

He proceeded to tell him what he had seen and what he and Seamus suspected. Not omitting a single detail about the beast, the eyes, the bear, the man. The draw he had felt to Grace as she invoked the Fae magic from within the earth, he chose to keep those feelings to himself.

"The only bear I have ever seen in these parts was the Dorcha," Brody spoke up first, "the night Faith and I did the ceremony in the dolmen. It's eyes glowed red, this beast who called itself Rowan?"

"Aye," Torin replied, confusion still filling his mind. "It was a bear. I am positive about that. I saw it clear as day. When he looked at me I saw his eyes. They nearly looked through me. He knew I was there."

"Do ye' think it's possible she invoked it? We banished it,

but we did not eliminate it entirely," Cormac spoke as he stepped toward Declan's desk.

"She wasn't trying to. If she did, it was by mistake," Torin explained as he took up for Grace at the sight of the anger on his father's face.

"Oh aye?" Declan glared at him, believing the half-Fae was trouble from the moment she arrived.

"Aye, I can confirm, so can Shay, and Cassidy. She was trying to perform a love spell for her true mate. It..." He paused, thinking through this portion of the story he had held back carefully. "It was working, summoning her mate," he sighed, "she is my mate."

Silence filled the room, Torin's brothers and father all looked at him. Seamus, unphased by this information waited for the others to process it.

"Fuck!" Brody was the first to speak.

After all these years, after all they had been through with Beth and Torin, they all had given up hope that Torin would ever find his mate.

"Torin?" Declan spoke next, unsure of how to go on, "she left with this Rowan?"

"Aye," Torin nodded.

"Cassidy is calling her now, but I doubt she will reach her," Seamus told them all.

"Do we truly believe that this could be the Dorcha?" Cormac asked. "I mean by mistake, could she really have invoked it by mistake?" Concern for his new wee one and Olivia filled his mind as he spoke.

"Stranger things have happened," Brody answered, shrugging.

"We need to find them," Declan said and stood from behind his desk. "Cormac, stay here with the lasses and your wee baby. Protect the Keep. We will go find them."

On the command the pack filed out of the room and the Keep. Shifting as they hit the woods, they each let out a howl.

Torin felt a sense of foreboding fill him. He didn't expect to find them. There would be a trail to follow, but he held little hope in his heart. Perhaps it was his years of grief over the loss of Beth that had turned him into such a pessimist, regardless of what it was, he didn't hold hope in his heart now.

GRACE WOKE THE NEXT MORNING, HER BODY SORE FROM SLEEPING on the cold stone ground in the cave that Rowan had taken her to. Looking around, as she sat up she saw no signs of him now. Her phone buzzed in her pocket, and as she pulled it out she saw the missed calls and texts from Cassidy.

She knew her friend would be worried about her when she didn't arrive back at the Keep last night. But she needed time to come up with a plan. They couldn't stay here. She couldn't stay here. Her life was in Dublin, sighing she realized how little she had planned for if the spell had actually worked. Hitting the call button on her phone she thought through her words carefully as the phone rang.

"Grace!" Cassidy's voice greeted her, "Where are you?" Her tone changed. "The pack spent the whole night looking for you."

"Shit, Cassidy. Tell them to call it off. I'm fine. I don't need them to get involved." She stretched and stood, making her way to the mouth of the cave and looking out into the morning light. "It worked! I found him!" Excitement coursed through Grace as she thought about Rowan.

"Grace, I need to tell you something," Cassidy's voice trailed off.

"What is it?" Her stomach churned. She could tell that her friend was hesitant to share what was on her mind.

"No, it's... I can't. But you need to come back here. Shay needs to speak with you. We need to see you, Grace," Cassidy pleaded with her.

"I can't, Rowan and I are going to…" she paused thinking through her words, "we are going to figure this out together."

"Rowan?" Cassidy asked, her curiosity piqued, she had heard the name last night. Torin had told her that this is what the bear shifter had called himself.

"Yes, he came to me last night, summoned by my spell." Grace didn't go on. She didn't have any other information to share. She didn't know the man, but she knew what she felt when they were together. "I have to go," Grace cleared her throat. Rowan came into view on the horizon, his toned muscular body glistening in the morning sun. He was still naked. The first order of business would be to get him clothes and find them a place to stay.

"Grace, wait—" Cassidy pleaded again.

Grace cutting her off went on, "I'm safe, it's fine. I'm sorry I had to cut our weekend short. I'll call you soon." Grace ended the call, she could hear Cassidy saying something as she pulled the phone from her ear, the word Dorcha made her raise an eyebrow. But Rowan stepped up to her, wrapped her in his arms and carried her back into the cave. All thoughts left her mind, and she smiled down at the man who held her in his arms.

"Grace," he said and nuzzled her neck, taking in the scent of the woman who had saved him from the hell he had been banished to.

"Rowan," she giggled. "I need to head to town. You can't keep running around naked."

"Oh aye? I plan to keep you naked with me here for as long as I can, sweet Grace," he purred in her ear.

"We can't, I need to return to Dublin. To my life. We can head there today." She squirmed in his arms as she spoke. Trying to keep herself clear headed as she felt his cock pushing against her.

"Grace," Rowan laid her back in his lap as he took a seat on the floor of the cave, looking down into her eyes.

He had spent the morning in the woods exploring, spying on the wolves as they searched the surrounding O'Gannigan lands for them. He had learned so much about this form, the power he now held. He couldn't leave, he had one thing on his mind, vengeance. He couldn't bear to let go of his sweet Grace, he needed to keep her with him. Here in Kerry, Dublin was out of the question. He dove into his mind, he had done this once before with Faith, he purred in his mind at the memories of the time he spent with her beneath the Keep.

He would feed her the images, the truth he needed her to believe. As he pushed forward into Grace's mind she gasped, the strange feeling of having him there caught her off guard. She could feel the darkness around the edges of what he was showing her, but she welcomed the connection between them. So pleased with how strong a bond they had.

"Rowan?" Her eyes were unseeing, her mind a swirl of magic and emotions.

"My sweet Grace." Cupping his hand he looked down into her face.

Feeding her one false memory after another. Before long she relaxed in his arms, her initial tension at having him invade her thoughts and mind melting away as she welcomed him in.

Coaxing her further he purred into her ear, "Master." Grace nodded at his word.

Her Fae blood called to him, he knew she would prove useful to his cause, and he would be sure not to break her as he had women in the past, he would be gentle with her. She deserved the world for saving him from the dark fate he had been living and he would make her his Queen as thanks.

Before long he pulled back from the depths of her mind, allowing time for the images and ideas he had planted there to take root and grow. He brushed his fingers down the side of her face, her skin so perfectly soft and smooth called to him and he craved her body beneath his.

"Rowan," she gasped as his hand brushed against her breast beneath her shirt.

"Mmm, sweet Grace," he purred into her ear. Kissing down the side of her neck.

She shifted in his lap, allowing him to lift her shirt off over her head. Rowan licked his lips and dove toward her, closing his mouth over her breast. Grace arched her back giving him better access to her as his hand slid down her stomach to the waistband of her jeans.

Her mind swirled with the idea that they could stay here in this place, she needed to please him, needed to make her Master happy. When his hand slipped into her jeans and found her clit all thoughts escaped her. Rowan, releasing her nipple from his mouth, laid Grace back onto the floor of the cave, pulling her jeans down over her hips. As he looked down on the naked woman that lay before him, his fangs slipped down from his gums and he imagined what it would be like to devour her whole.

Grace arched her back again, wanting to feel his hands on her, his mouth and tongue all over her skin. Rowan shifted overtop of Grace positioning himself between her thighs, bending toward her, as he took her into his mouth. The sweet taste of her pussy covered his tongue and both moaned.

"Are you going to come for me, sweet thing?" he murmured the words against her inner thigh as he trailed his fingers down her soaking slit.

"May I, Master?" she cooed to him.

Rowan smiled, knowing the false memories he fed her were thoroughly taking root in her mind, by her response.

"Aye, come for me, Grace. I want to taste your sweet honey on my tongue." He finished speaking as he closed his mouth over her again.

Squeezing her eyes closed, Grace saw stars of magic in her mind, she embraced the feeling and let it wash over her as she came for her Master, squirming beneath his touch. Rowan shifted himself to his knees, pushing the tip of his cock to her entrance and then slowly pushing himself forward into her. Rowan tossed his head back and roared as he entered her.

"MINE," HE BENT OVER GRACE'S BODY AND WHISPERED INTO HER ear, "only mine."

"Mmm," she nodded, her eyes flying open as she felt the sharpness of his fangs graze against the side of her neck. "Master?" she gasped out the word, confusion filling her mind.

He coaxed her body with his, pushing into her mind, feeding her images of her accepting him in this way. Her Fae blood called to him deeply, he craved it, wanting it coursing through his veins. As Grace relaxed beneath Rowan's body he smiled against her neck. Driving himself into her further. Not wishing to hurt her, he needed to bring her to the edge of her release, he closed his eyes. Focusing on his inner beast, allowing the bear inside him to float to the surface. Claws extended from his hands, sliding down her arms, the faint lines of blood blooming over her skin.

Grace cried out, tightening down around Rowan's cock buried in her pussy. As she floated toward the edge of her orgasm, she felt the pin pricks of his fangs breaking the skin at the side of her neck.

"Fuck!" Rowan ground out the word, his cock throbbed, his balls tightened against him. The taste of the magic in her veins coating his tongue drove him nearly mad.

The urge to rip out her throat and take every last drop tore through his chest and he bucked inside her. Both could feel the buzzing of the magic in the space between them, in their veins. Grace's eyes flew open wide, and she looked lifelessly up at the ceiling of the cave. When a claw grazed against her clit she exploded around Rowan still buried deep inside her.

His deep laugh filled the room as he continued to drain her

lifeblood, it coated his throat, his eyes flared red, and when Grace looked into them, she was lost to this man. This creature. As the Fae magic filled him he toyed with it, allowing it to expand his own powers. He dove into Grace's mind again, weaving a beautiful illusion for her. They lay naked, together on the floor as he pleased her, promising her the world, making her his Queen.

"Soon," he purred in her ear. Licking the last drops of her blood from his lips. "You shall be my Queen. We will rule this land and feed freely. First," he pushed images of the wolves dying at his hand into her mind, "we must eliminate those who wish to pull us apart.

"Yes, Master," she smiled up at him, feeling weak and hazy, her hand fell to her side as she tried to lift it to his cheek.

Exhaustion took her over, she didn't understand what she was feeling, why she was so tired suddenly. The memory of him draining her magic from her slipping out of her mind as he delved into it and planted more of what he wished her to see there.

"Rowan," she mouthed his name as her head lolled to the side.

Rowan stood, looking down at the lifeless body beneath him. His veins thrummed with the magic he had stolen from her. He smiled, fangs sliding down over his lower lip. As he shifted, his massive paws landed on the stone floor next to her. Bursting forth from the cave he had one destination in mind, he needed to feed. Needed to find the perfect victim. The blood he now craved was that which would allow him to continue to remain immortal.

HUMANS WERE UNDERRATED, THEY PROVIDED SO MUCH FOR THOSE of his kind. The damned wolves had made it their mission to protect them, like sheep in the fields being guarded by dogs. He growled at the thought. He would not allow them to interfere this time. The Fae magic he now had an endless supply of would give him all he needed. Creeping through the still dim morning light he tossed his nose into the air, the scent of fresh blood filled it. The sound of a heartbeat in the distance met his ears. A snarl spread over his muzzle.

At last, he saw her, the small slip of a woman in the field just ahead. A basket hanging from her arm, her long, golden locks trailing down her back. She smelled so sweet, her heartbeat calling to him. Crouching low he crept through the tall grass toward her. The winter air around him, he could see puffs of her breath around her face. When she looked up at the rustling sound as he approached, he knew it was too late. She had no chance of escaping him. It had been so long, too long since he had last fed. Lunging forward his back paws pushed from the ground, and he collided with her body.

The scream ripped from her throat fell silent as his claws tore open her chest. Looking down at her still beating heart he licked his lips, driving his muzzle forward into the broken bones of her chest and devoured it. They would know, he thought to himself as he made his way back to Grace. The wolves would hear of the woman with the missing heart, and they would know he had returned. Dorcha, once more, he would rule these lands, feeding his hunger, and he would kill each and every last one of them.

CHAPTER
FIVE

TORIN TOSSED and turned in his bed all morning. Their night had proved fruitless. His inner turmoil had him torn the entire time. He didn't want this, but he couldn't deny the pull he had felt in the clearing. Beth had been gone for so long, his love for her still remained and it had hardened his heart to the truth. He wasn't searching for his mate, but fate had brought her here and he could not allow her to be with another. The beast he had seen with her in the dolmen was no mere mortal, the darkness he had seen and felt told him the truth of it.

Grace was in danger, and while he did not desire to love her, to hold her, or claim her. He did not wish her harm and knew the pack had been right to make the decision to search for her. They would save her, but what did that mean for him, what did it mean for his mate?

"Grace?" he called her name into the empty space of the room around him, "where are you?"

His father was convinced that this being he had seen was the Dorcha returned. He was not yet convinced. He couldn't fathom that his mate had been taken by the lifeform they had for so many centuries battled and banished at last. The thought of it turned his stomach and facing that as the truth would tear him apart. What cruel fate would do this to him? If this was his fate, if he was at last presented with his fated mate, only to lose her the same night to the darkness. What twisted destiny would this be?

"Torin," he had hardly slept and as he rolled onto his side, he saw Seamus standing in the doorway. "We need to talk."

"Aye, I'm coming," he said as he rose and followed his brother through the Keep to their father's study.

"Cassidy spoke to Grace this morning. She is alive, but she would not hear of returning here," Seamus told the group.

"We have word from town of a missing woman. She went out to forage this morn' and failed to return," Cormac told them all.

"It could mean anything, not be related at all," Declan told his sons. "Many women have vanished from town over the centuries since we banished the Dorcha. They leave town and go in search of fun in the big city. Do we have any proof there is foul play?"

"Nay," Cormac told his father.

"We must wait for proof, we cannot hunt for a figment of our imaginations," Torin spoke up at last. "If Grace has summoned the Dorcha it will show itself before long. We wait, we plan. But we do not need to jump to conclusions." He was sure of one thing, Grace had left with an evil being, it had her in its grasp. If it was in fact the Dorcha still remained unknown.

His three brothers nodded their agreement, his father looked less convinced. "There is a search party for the missing woman?"

***

"Aye, the police and the townsfolk are planning to set out and search the fields. There is fear she was injured in the woods and is in need of medical attention, unable to call for help," Cormac told them.

"We shall join them, on foot. Join the party and render our

aid as we would to any other, Dorcha or not. We have always protected these parts. Our family is bound by honor to continue to do so." They all nodded, none of them had gotten much rest, but their father was right. When the townsfolk needed them they stepped up, this would be the same.

They searched for hours, long after the sun set. The police refused to call off the search, the fear of winter weather causing an already injured woman to become hypothermic drove them on.

Torin was the one to find her, the cover of darkness had given them the opportunity to shift and search the woods as wolves. Their heightened senses providing an added benefit. The smell of blood led him right to her. He tossed his head back and howled for the pack.

Ann Green's body lay at his feet, her blood soaking the grass around her. Seeing the lights of the search party in the distance he signaled to them.

"Here, I have her! Here!" Torin yelled at them.

Her chest torn open, heart missing, it meant one thing. As his brothers emerged from the woods the police and her husband approached across the field.

"Dorcha," Brody was the first to say what they all now knew to be true.

"Aye." Torin's heart sank. His mate was in the hands of a monster.

Having given all he could to the cause to find the poor woman from the village he strode off toward the woods. He had his answer and it meant one thing. He needed to find her now. He could not wait any longer. Grace was in grave danger. Cloaked at last in the trees from the men in the field he shifted and took off. He would search all night again if he must. But he was determined to find her.

Dawn broke over the crest of the hill he sat on. The long night had led him back to this place. He had been here twice before, one hundred years apart. Whimpering, he lay on the cold grass and closed his eyes. He needed to think, needed to come up with an explanation for all his emotions surrounding Grace and Beth.

Duty bound him to save her from the Dorcha. To save them all from it. However, he felt duty bound him to Beth's memory as well. This place was thick with it. The land where she took her last breath. Shifting, he rolled onto his back. Put his arms behind his head and looked up at the sky as the sun rose. Images of the two women collided in his mind. The night he had first spent with Beth in the Keep when she arrived with Faith, the day she was betrothed to Brody. The images of Grace's face as she sat at the dinner table in the great hall with his family as he watched from the top of the stairs.

He could see the similarities between them, the same heart shaped face. The same hair color. Perhaps his attraction to Grace was simply that she reminded him of Beth. Denial was still filling his mind, even though he had felt the truth of the magic, even though he had told Seamus and Cassidy, as well as his father, that he believed Grace was his mate. It was so easy to deny it. It would be so easy to walk away. No, he thought. It wouldn't be easy. It would be hell. It would be like the years of hell he had lived through as he mourned Beth. He could not inflict that on himself again. A self-inflicted wound to his heart is all that it would be.

"Torin?" Seamus's voice reached his ears. The memory of being in this same opening with his brother so long ago the night he had last returned here filled his mind.

"Aye?" He sat up and watched Seamus approach him.

"Any luck?" Seamus asked, taking a seat on the grass next to Torin.

"No, nothing. There is no sign of them at all. I searched all night." He lay his head back on his arms and looked up into the sky once more.

"Why are you here?" Seamus was blunt with his brother.

"I needed to speak to Beth," Torin said and sighed.

"Aye, did she have the answers?" Seamus smiled at the idea of seeking answers from the dead.

"She always has the answers I need. Not necessarily the ones I want, however." Torin continued to watch the sky. "I need to find Grace. I need to figure out what this is between us and go from there. We need to kill the Dorcha and end this once and for all. I just can't get over the idea of her being with that," he searched for the right word, "beast. We need to save her. These feelings I have. I can't sort them out. I need to put them aside. We have to focus on the facts." He sighed.

"Really? Do we really need to focus on the facts and not your emotions? Emotions can play a big role in this. I can help you with them, I can help you sort them out. Just talk to me, Torin." Seamus yearned for his brother to open up to him.

"I don't know, Shay, a heart to heart doesn't feel like it's really the answer here." Torin didn't go on. He didn't know what else to say.

"Tell me what Beth said," Seamus pushed him.

"That it is time to let her go." Torin felt tears stinging the backs of his eyes as he choked out the words. "That it has been long enough. I don't need to keep putting myself through this."

"She said all that?" Seamus began to wonder if talking to the dead was more useful than he thought.

"Aye, she has a lot to say a lot of the time." Torin was used to talking to Beth. The time they had together had been short, but it had been spent talking for hours through the night. Among being in bed together, they had a connection he couldn't deny.

"But you don't agree?" Seamus knew Torin didn't, he knew his brother still hung onto the pain in his heart that he felt at the loss of Beth so long ago. They had been together in this clearing that night. He had heard the pain in his howls, the pain in his voice, saw it in his eyes.

Seamus remembered the pain that he had felt when he thought he was losing Cassidy last year. The months they had been separated, the time they spent apart. It had killed him. But he knew she was still alive, knew she was still breathing, her heart still beating. Beth's life had been snuffed out. It had been ended here on this very ground. This pain was different, it must be far worse than what he felt. What Torin felt that night, what he has been feeling for so many years.

"Torin," Seamus searched for the words, for a moment he considered asking Beth himself what he should say, "I'm sorry. The pain you've been through. What you've felt, I can only imagine how horrible it can be. I know when I thought I lost Cassidy it was hell. Truly losing her, I cannot fathom how hard that would be." He knew he was contradicting himself, knew what he was saying wasn't making sense.

"Shay," Torin searched through his memories, looking for the right words to explain it, "it is like losing a part of yourself."

Seamus nodded, he got that. He understood what losing a part of himself would feel like. His chest felt tight.

They lay on the grass in silence as the sun rose over them in the sky. Both thought through the things they had said. The things they felt. Neither of them knew what the answer was for Torin. At last Torin stood, holding his hand out to Seamus.

"We should get back," Torin told him.

They shifted once they were in the trees. The journey back to the Keep was silent for them both. Neither of them thought of Grace or Beth. Both just enjoyed the sounds of the birds in the trees and the wilderness around them. Being wolves, being in their true form, it brought each of them some peace in an otherwise loud world. The answers Torin needed would come in time. Whether he got them from Beth or from within himself, Seamus and he both knew that they were coming.

CHAPTER
SIX

GRACE WOKE AS NIGHT FELL, the crackle of a fire drawing her attention to Rowan sitting by her side.

"You're awake," he spoke to her as she sat up.

"Aye," her head ached, and she placed her hand on her forehead wondering how she had managed to sleep the day away. "I slept all day?"

"Aye, I think you needed it." She nodded at him. The spell must have taken more out of her than she realized. Her memory of the morning they spent together was a haze.

Looking down at her arms she saw the scratches that had begun to heal there, his claws, had caused the damage while they made love. She smiled at the thought. He had been more beast than man when they were together this time, his bear coming out.

"You need to eat." Waving his hand a plate of food appeared in her lap. Grace gawked at him. This was Fae magic, she had seen it before, could feel it in the air around them.

"What?" Grace had wished for so many years that she could summon this amount of Fae magic to her. She had never been able, being only half-blood. "How?" She scrunched her nose as she tilted her head to the side and took him in. Realizing she knew nothing about the man she had summoned to her she wondered now if he were truly Fae.

"Eat," he commanded her.

Grace did as she was told, but her mind still swirled with questions. "How do you have Fae magic?"

"I can teach you many things, Grace. I will make you my Queen and we will rule over these lands." He grinned at her, the mirth in his eyes excited her.

"Aye? You can teach me to use my Fae magic, at will?" Rowan nodded at her, and she beamed as she lifted a piece of fruit from her plate. "Rowan, where are you from? What are you? How old are you?"

His laughter was music to her ears. "So many questions, my sweet Grace. In time, all will be clear. But I will tell you one story tonight."

"Nearly one thousand years ago magic stirred in the earth, in the lands that would become known as Kerry. I emerged from the primordial ooze. More beast than man, I roamed these lands. Watching for centuries as the magical beings who ruled the land came and fell. I learned many things. Met many beings. As time passed my powers grew, but so did others' hatred of me, jealousy is a powerful thing."

Grace nodded as he spoke, she understood what he was saying, she knew the legends of the Fae. Knew many hated their strength and at last they were forced into hiding, over time humans forgot the truth and believed them mere stories.

Rowan went on, "I was banished, unjustly. Forced into the earth, to live in the in-between for centuries. You saved me, you summoned me forth into this time and place. Your siren's call woke me from a slumber and here I am. I have been called many things over the course of my time. You, my dear sweet Grace, are the first to see me in my true form, hear my true name, know my truest of hearts."

"Rowan..." She set her plate aside, her belly full, and her desire to be in his arms only increasing as he spoke. "I'm so sorry. Having been banished from my own kind to live among humans, alone for centuries, I, too, know the hurt you have felt."

Placing her hand on the side of his face, she leaned in and kissed him softly, the metallic tang of blood filled her mouth, and she jerked back, eyes wide.

"I'm sorry, for I fed in my other form. Do I offend?" She shook her head as he spoke. Not wanting to give him the wrong impression she leaned into him again, her heart ached for him and his tale of loneliness.

His body, pressed against hers near the heat of the dying fire, made her want to be with him again.

"Master?" she cooed to him, the memories of their time together driving her to use the title.

It was clear by the way he looked down at her that he was pleased that she chose to address him in this way without coaxing.

"Sweet Grace, we have plans for the night. Ravishing you is on my list. First, we must head to town. I fear I am not presentable in my present state," he said, while motioning to his still naked body. Grace blushed.

"Aye, we need to get you clothes and, rather I suspect, familiarize you with the twenty-first century." Slipping her cell phone from her pocket she presented it to him. "We call it a phone. It is used to communicate."

Rowan raised a brow, taking the small thing from her hand, and turning it over in his own. Grace smiled at the confusion on his face, patting his leg.

"I'll head to town to fetch you clothes. Then we shall return together and explore?" She wanted to teach him about her time, her life just as much as she wanted to learn more about his history. "We really should find a place to stay, not here in this cave."

Rowan growled low in his chest, he would not leave Kerry and go to Dublin as she had previously asked.

"We cannot live here, in the wilderness. I am not a shifter," Grace pleaded her case.

"I can provide for you. I shall hunt myself and…" He waved his hand. The space around her twinkled to life, as Grace turned in a circle the cave changed from dark, damp stone, to opulent apartment.

Outdated as it was, she was amazed, the Fae magic she felt in the air had her curious again how he was doing such things. When she turned to face him again, he waved his hand over his body, a black t-shirt similar to her own and jeans appeared over his naked body. Rowan took her face into his hands and kissed her deeply, brushing against her mind as he had before. Coaxing her to let him in, opening her mind to his.

He knew his capabilities only lasted so long, knew that her mind, powerful as it was, would reveal the truth to her given the appropriate amount of time. He wouldn't be able to keep her under his thumb for long in this form, though, the more of her Fae power he absorbed the stronger his compulsion abilities would grow.

Grace rubbed herself against his thigh, moaning as he kissed her and fed her images of them together. Rowan regretted not creeping into her dreams while she slept, when her mind was more malleable. But she relaxed in his arms and welcomed him now.

Grace could feel the coaxing sensation against that place in her mind that only she could reach. Could feel Rowan brush up against her memories of them together. She never imagined that having her mate at last would be so intimate, that they would share such a bond. It filled her with joy and she opened herself to him fully.

Lifting her in his arms he carried her to the bed he had summoned into the cave. Laying her back on it, he looked down over the form of the woman he had before him. The memories of so many he had taken in the past filled his mind. None compared to what being with Grace was like in this form.

He waved his hand and Grace gasped as both of their clothes disappeared. He knew he would need more of her Fae blood soon if he were going to keep up these abilities. Grace looked up into Rowan's eyes and he looked down at her. The reverence she saw in them made her heart soar. Reaching out her arms to him she welcomed the feeling of his warm body over hers. When their skin touched the magic of it coursed through her. A moment of darkness filled her mind and she cried out in fear.

Rowan, sensing he had pushed too deep pulled back, he needed to not scare her from him. Reaching between their bodies he took hold of his cock and rubbed the head of himself up and down her slit. She was slick with need and her appreciative moan filled his ears.

"My sweet Grace, my Queen," he purred into her ear as he slid forward into her pussy.

"Rowan," she called to him as he entered her. She needed to feel his hands on her, his mouth. Needed their bodies to be connected in this way.

Pushing in and out of her heat he watched her eyes fill with pleasure, he wanted to please her just as much as he wanted to take his pleasure from her. The gift she had granted him was something he could not repay. Shifting onto the bed, kneeling between her legs for a better position he drove home into her, to the hilt.

Continuing to ride her, Rowan bent and pressed kisses to the side of her face, trailing down her neck and collarbone, at last he found her breast and sucked a nipple into his mouth. Grazing his teeth over the sensitive flesh.

Grace cried out, she needed this, needed more. "Please," she begged.

"Please?" He looked down into her eyes, raising his brow.

"Master, take me. Give me what I need," Grace pled with him. Lost in the moment.

"Mmm, I think perhaps it is time for you to please me." Winking at her he rose from the bed.

The empty feeling that overtook Grace made her whine. She wanted him inside her again. Rowan held a hand out to Grace, helping her from the opulent bed and then guiding her to her knees in front of him. The soft fur of the rug he had conjured brushed against her knees as she knelt before him. His cock bobbed in front of her, making her lick her lips.

"Open your mouth," brushing his thumb over her lower lip as he issued the command, Grace nodded.

She wanted to please him, wanted to do as he asked. She knew at that moment, this man, the beast, her Master, she would do anything for him. The feeling startled her, where the thought came from she wasn't sure, but she felt it in her heart.

As she parted her lips Rowan took hold of the back of her head and pushed himself forward between them. The feeling of her warm tongue sliding down his shaft had him growling his pleasure.

"Good girl," he purred to her, "suck me."

Grace nodded, pushing herself up on her knees for a better position. She arched her back and pushed her breasts out, hoping to entice him forward to her. She wanted to feel his hands on her breasts as she pleased him in this way. Still holding her head in his hands Rowan pushed himself further into her mouth, brushing against the back of her throat and smiling at the power he felt when she gagged on him.

Suddenly his demeanor changed, Grace could feel the shift in the space around them, the air thick with it. Rowan slammed himself home into her throat, claiming her mouth for his own pleasure. Rowan didn't know what had driven him to this point but he needed her to know he was the true Master of her body, her mind. He needed her to bow to him, to worship at his feet.

Continuing to force himself down her throat he growled, the power of the control coursing through him. As he swelled in her mouth Grace could tell he was going to come, he wasn't going to please her, her own needs were long forgotten.

"Choke on me, take it all, everything I give you," his command was harsh.

As hot spurts of cum hit her tongue he continued to use her mouth, his claws extending and digging into her scalp, Grace winced.

Rowan delved forward into her mind, pushing past her barriers and invading it. He fed her images of him behind her, overtop of her, of her bowing at his feet. "Master," he cooed to her, "I am your Master."

Grace's eyes glossed over as she was bombarded with the images. She tried to nod her agreement. He was her Master. He was in control, she would turn herself over to him, body, mind, and soul. Stepping back from her, Rowan looked down at Grace, her chin coated in his cum.

"Bow." The one word reverberated through her body. Falling forward onto the ground she stretched her arms out in front of her, her nose pressed to the ground.

"You will be my Queen, but you will recognize that I am King. In all things. If you accept this, I shall allow you to rule by my side," Rowan bent as he spoke looking at the form of the naked woman bowing before him. Her perfectly curved hips and ass in the air.

She was a miracle, he knew the truth of it, he knew she did not summon him for his strength. She craved his approval and that would play so well into his plans.

"Rise," he granted her this release, Grace lifted her eyes to Rowan's.

Still kneeling before him she took in his form before her. The toned muscles of his chest, she still needed, still craved more of him. He had found his release in her and left her wanting more.

"Master," she said and pressed herself down on her thighs. The heat and slickness between her legs made her hungry for her own release.

"My sweet saving Grace." Holding his hand out to her he helped her to her feet. Turning her back to him, his long fingers splayed over her shoulders. Brushing the hair from the nape of her neck he licked the soft flesh there. Seeing her pulse, the power flowing through her veins calling to him. Pushing her toward the bed, he bent her over it and forced himself home into her with no preparation.

Grace screamed out her approval, pushing her ass into the air for him to take her pussy. She needed to feel him deep inside her now.

"Ride me," Rowan's hands settled onto her hips, and he allowed Grace to set the pace.

She bounced on his cock, pushing herself further and further down on him each time. Buried so deeply in her, his balls pressed against her ass. He groaned, he needed to feed on her again, he could feel the power in his veins waning, but he would not hurt her to do so.

As Grace found a steady rhythm, he leaned into her. Her hand slipped down between her legs, and she expertly circled her clit, matching her own pace. Fingers brushing over her pale skin, his claws extending again he pulled them down over her back from her shoulders to her ass. The blood bloomed and he licked his lips, bending as she continued to ride him he licked each long wound from the base of her spine to her shoulder. Grace reveled in the feel of his tongue on her skin, the heat of it.

The sting of his claws flaying her back open had been a mere inconvenience, the pleasure she derived from him as she continued to please herself fogging her mind to the reality of what he had done. Rowan slowly trailed his tongue over each of the slashes in her back, taking what he needed from her, not a single drop of her magical blood was wasted.

When Grace looked back over her shoulder there was a gleam in his eyes, they flickered red, and she flinched back from him for the merest of moments. Rowan drove himself home into her. "Come for me," he ordered her roughly.

Grace cried out, finding her release, forgetting what she thought she saw in his eyes. No doubt, she told herself, a trick of the flickering fire. As she collapsed forward onto the bed she could feel strong arms come around her, lifting her to his chest, Rowan carried her to the side of the bed. Suddenly, she was exhausted again, she had spent the day sleeping, yet she could hardly keep her eyes open.

Rowan tucked her under the covers and curled beside her, playing in the realms of her mind, he fed her dream after dream. At last, when he knew she would not rouse, he lifted her wrist, the quick slash of a claw over her perfectly unflawed skin releasing the blood he so deeply craved. Closing his mouth over her wrist he drained all he could, feeling the power of the Fae magic coursing through his veins. Laughter filled the cave and Grace turned, heavy lidded eyes fluttering open.

"Rowan?" she yawned.

"Aye?" He kissed her eyelids closed and looked down as her lashes fluttered on her cheeks.

She was gone again, the veil of exhaustion winning out over her desire for answers. Grace dreamt then, images of her and Rowan together flooding her mind.

Rowan needed to feed. He needed the lifeblood that would continue to sustain him. While he hated leaving Grace, he knew he must. Creeping from the cave he went in search of his next victim.

CHAPTER
SEVEN

TORIN AND SEAMUS had returned to the Keep. The rest of the pack was sitting at the breakfast table in the great hall when they entered. They took their seats and all of them sat silently eating breakfast for a time.

"Poor Ann," Gwen said as she sat at the table in the hall surrounded by her sons, Declan sat at the head of the table.

"Tis' the Dorcha, of this we can be sure. We must stop this before the village suffers." Declan's words were harsh. Torin's insides twisted as his father thought only of the townsfolk.

He didn't consider Torin and Grace, once again he and his heart were brushed aside for the greater good of the pack and those they were sworn to protect. He stood, the legs of his chair scraping against the stone floor as he did. "This is bullshite!" he raged. He couldn't hold it back any longer.

The three faces of his brother's turned to him. Brody stood and crossed to him, he knew Faith and Brody had a history with the Dorcha. Faith had been taken and tortured, he knew his brother wanted to protect his mate as much as he wanted to protect his. He had been turning the idea of Grace over in his mind all night. The magic had called to him, told him the truth of it, his hardened heart had begun to soften, and he was willing to see the truth. The conversation he had with Seamus this morning had already begun to lead him down this path.

"Torin, we are going to find her. We will save her from it, we will not allow it to take her from you." Brody's words reached him as he was about to exit the hall.

Feet freezing on the spot he turned and looked into his brother's eyes. "I cannot do this again." He nearly collapsed. The pain he suffered for centuries, his inability to let Beth go. It all crashed down on him at this moment. Declan took in the exchange between his sons, realizing his misstep.

"Torin, we will save Grace. She will not be lost to the Dorcha." He stood, crossing to his son.

The space between them, the gulf that he had opened up so many years ago when he acted in a way he believed to be justified, it felt so massive now. Centuries had passed, but no healing had been done.

"Son," he said as he placed his hand on Torin's shoulder, "I have never said I'm sorry for the past. I was wrong. I will not allow you to suffer again, we will find her."

Torin looked into his father's eyes, this admission from him, it was the first and undoubtedly the last he would ever receive. He tried not to let it eat at him that it had taken so long and that it wasn't a real apology. He said that he had never said he was sorry, he didn't actually say it now.

"I am to trust you now, because you can admit after three centuries that you were wrong?" Torin spat the words, they felt thick and sour on his tongue. "You killed Beth! An innocent woman, a member of the village we are sworn to protect! Not once did you come to speak to me. You made no effort to see things my way. To hear us out, to reason with us." He fumed, pacing the hall then.

"Torin, what more do you want from me? I cannot go back and bring the poor girl back!"

"You coward, you didn't even have the balls to do it

yourself! You ordered Shay to do it! Now you are going to play the victim and say you can't do anything about it because it's in the past." Torin spun on his father, fire filled his eyes, and he fought the urge to shift here in the Keep.

"I…" Declan didn't go on. He had nothing to say in his defense. They all knew that Torin was right. This had been the elephant in the room for three centuries.

"I'm going to look for Grace. I refuse to stand by and wait for her body to be the one we find in a field next." He stormed from the Keep. He had been up for over twenty-four hours. He knew he needed to rest. He had returned home for just that. But the argument with his father had him back at it again, he would find her. He must.

Voices erupted in the hall as he slammed the door shut behind him. As he reached the woods he shifted, hearing the sound of footsteps behind him he turned. Seamus had his right flank, Brody his left. The three headed into the woods to search for any sign of Rowan and Grace. Their search turned up nothing. They had spent the entire day and night searching yet again. As the sun rose over the horizon three wolves crouched, gathered on an outcropping of rocks looking down over the town.

Each sighed, exhaustion taking them over from two days and nights spent searching high and low for Grace. A commotion drew their attention to the edge of town where people could be seen gathering. The sound of a woman's scream sliced through the morning air. The three brothers took off down the face of the cliff toward the town, sticking to the shadows.

As they approached the border of the woods they shifted forms and quickly headed across the field on foot. The sight of a woman's body came into view between the onlookers.

"What's happened?" Torin asked a man standing to his right.

He knew from the looks of the woman that the Dorcha had struck again during the night. Her chest, torn open, heart gone, it was clear to him.

"She was found like this, just like Ann. What monster is among us?" the man from town said, his voice shaky.

"I need to tell the others," Brody told Seamus and Torin as he turned and headed back to the Keep.

Torin and Seamus, both knowing the truth of the mystery that was the woman's body, left the scene. They needed to get to the Dorcha before it killed again and kill it would. Endless death would cast its shadow over Kerry until it was stopped.

THREE WEEKS LATER

MORE THAN A DOZEN WOMEN HAD TURNED UP DEAD ACROSS KERRY over the course of the previous three weeks. Grace knew nothing of what was happening. She had been holed up with Rowan in the comfort of their cave. Her phone battery had long ago died, and she had no contact with the outside world.

She rolled on the bed, turning to see Rowan sitting on the edge of it. So often she had woken this way, finding him awake already for the day. "Penny for your thoughts?" she asked him, reaching her arm out and trailing it down his back.

"Just thinking of you, my sweet Grace," he told her.

Standing from the edge of the bed he waited, they had fallen into a routine each morning. Grace rose and slipped from the bed, falling to her knees then bowing before him on the stone ground.

"Rise," he commanded her. Waving his hand, her nightie and his sweatpants disappeared. He had been getting the hang of this century and of her magic.

Grace rose to her knees, her hands laying palm up on her thighs as she bowed her head to her chest and waited for him to approach her. Fingers gripped her chin and tilted her face up. Looking up into Rowan's eyes, she parted her lips and accepted the gift he was granting her. She took his cock in her mouth, running her tongue up and down his shaft then sucking him in fully and swallowing him.

"Mmm, Grace, your mouth feels incredible on me. Don't stop," he told her as he twisted his fingers in her hair and guided her further down onto his cock.

She could feel her own spit running down her chin, tears sliding down her cheeks as he forced himself deeper into her mouth. She loved every second of it, this had been how she woke up each morning. Pleasing her Master and if she could do this for the rest of her life she would be in heaven.

Rowan pulled himself from her mouth and grabbed the base of his cock, his cum shooting from the end of it onto her tongue as she held it out, happy to receive what he was giving her. Looking down at her breasts they were also coated with his cum. Rowan smiled, she was his, he had sufficiently marked her repeatedly. He would continue to do so.

Never able to get enough of her he jerked his cock again in his fist, hard and ready for more he motioned for her to get on the bed. Grace turned, crawling onto the bed, her ass in the air as she leaned forward onto her elbows. Rowan drove forward into her. It was her turn, she licked her lips, his cum still covering them. She was sticky with it.

"Mmm, dirty little whore, aren't you? Just waiting for me to fuck you each morning." Rowan took a fistful of her hair and jerked her head back, arching her back and pulling her backward onto his cock as he slipped in and out of her pussy.

"Yes, Master." His words made her feel a tingle of pleasure spreading through her belly.

Rowan's free hand smacked Grace's ass, then he slid it down

over her hip to her clit. He ran his fingers over the bundle of nerves bringing Grace closer to the edge of her climax. The hand in her hair slid down her back, claws extending and digging into her skin, fresh lines of blood appeared on her back. He bent and ran his tongue over them. Letting the Fae magic fill him as he continued to fuck her. Grace could feel the pressure of Rowan pushing forward into her mind as he filled her pussy. The emotion she felt at having this bond with him, mixed with the pleasure of having him use her body, pushed her over the edge and she came. Rowan could feel her tighten around him, feel the slickness of her cum coating him.

Tossing his head back he roared as he found his release again, filling her with his cum. Grace fell forward onto the bed, rolling onto her back. Rowan looked down at her, her face and breasts still covered in his cum. He watched it seeping from her. He smiled a wicked smile at her. Waving his hand a plate of fruit appeared in the bed next to Grace, she smiled and picked up a grape popping it into her mouth.

"Thank you, Master," she purred as she ate her fruit.

Rowan couldn't have been more thrilled with how well he had her trained, these past three weeks had proved useful. As Grace relaxed back on the bed and ate her plate of fruit he headed for the entrance of the cave. He needed to hunt, needed to feed.

As Cassidy listened to the voice-mail message telling her the inbox was full she tossed her phone onto the bed and turned to Seamus. Shaking her head, she watched his face fall. They had been attempting to track Grace for weeks and turned up nothing. Unsure if she was even still in Kerry at this point.

"I'm sorry." Seamus rubbed Cassidy's back, knowing her concern for her friend was causing her pain.

"No, I'm sorry. What about Torin? What about all these

women? They didn't deserve this, and I could have prevented it all." Cassidy sighed.

Torin listened to their exchange, he didn't blame Cassidy, she didn't know that the spell Grace had confided in her about would come to pass in this way.

"Cassidy, you couldn't have known. Grace couldn't have known," Torin made an attempt to console her.

"Aye," Seamus agreed.

"Where are they?" Cassidy sighed, her eyes filling with tears. "I'm worried about Grace. I'm scared." Seamus took her in his arms.

"It's okay. We will find her..." Seamus trailed off. A thought occurred to him. "Fuck! I can't believe I didn't think of it sooner," he jumped up from the couch in his living room and dashed out of the apartment.

Torin and Cassidy looked at each other, confusion covering their faces. They both ran from the apartment, following Seamus through the Keep. Skidding to a stop as he entered his father's study, Torin saw Seamus standing at Declan's desk, a book open in front of him as he flipped through the pages.

"Cass, did Grace leave her bag here?" He glanced up as she and Torin entered the room.

"Yes, it's in the guest room, she left everything here," Cassidy told him.

"Why? What are you thinking?" Torin asked as he came around to the side of the desk and glanced down at the page Seamus stopped on.

"Scrying. We did it to find Faith. I don't know how none of us thought of it sooner. Cass, go see what you can find, hairbrush, something along those lines." Seamus picked the book up and headed out of the study.

Torin's heart raced, there was hope. They had a chance to find her, something to help them in their tireless search.

"Torin, find Brody and Da' they know how to do the spell," Seamus told him as he followed him into the hall.

As he raced across it and up the staircase to find his father and brother, he couldn't stop thinking that this was it. This was the answer. Nearly colliding with Cassidy, as she came from an open door with a bag in her hands, he saw the look on her face. It mirrored his own, their thoughts the same. This was their chance to get her back.

"Brody!" He banged on the door to his brother's apartment.

"Aye," Brody opened the door, the look on Torin's face catching him off guard. "What's wrong?"

"We need your help, there is a spell. Shay said you used it to find Faith when the Dorcha took her." Brody's eyes widened.

"Shite, why didn't we think of it sooner!" Brody pulled the door closed behind him as he stepped into the hall. "We need a crystal, Da' should have what we need. I'll find him. Do you have something of Grace's?"

"Cassidy is on it. She and Seamus are in the hall. Meet us there," Torin told Brody then rushed back to the hall and saw Cassidy rifling through Grace's bag.

"Here," she said and nearly flung the hairbrush at his chest as he approached.

"How does this work?" Torin asked Seamus as he took the proffered hairbrush in his hand.

"We will use a crystal and a map, there is a spell here and it will lead you to her," Seamus said and pushed the book across the table toward Torin.

As he read the page he studied the words of the spell carefully, committing them to memory. He needed to make sure he said this exactly as it was written. He knew how Druid magic worked and Grace's errors in her own spell were proof of that.

Declan and Brody descended the stairs and came to stand

with the other three. Torin looked up from the book lying open before him and his eyes met his father's. The two hadn't spoken since the morning a few weeks prior when he accused him of being a coward, even though Declan had at last admitted he was wrong about Beth. The tension between them made Torin tense when his father offered him a crystal tied with a piece of ribbon. Torin nodded, waiting for any advice Brody or Declan had to offer. Seamus had explained the spell and he felt he had an understanding of how it worked.

"Is there a trick to it at all?" He turned to Brody, ignoring his father's pleading look.

"No, not that I found. I simply said the spell and the crystal did the rest. You need to wrap a piece of her hair around the stone first," Brody pointed to the hairbrush Torin had set down on the table.

Doing as he was told Torin pulled a piece of hair from the brush and wound it around the crystal in his hand. Focusing on the spell in his mind again, he looked down at the map Seamus unfolded before him.

Looking down over the map of Kerry he studied it closely. "Do we get more than one chance at this? What if she isn't in Kerry?"

"Aye, we can expand to the country if she isn't here. But we need it to be as precise as we can." Declan told him, "The smaller the area the more accurately we can pinpoint a spot on the map."

Torin nodded, still not willing to provide his father with a response. Perhaps when all of this was over the two could start healing the rift between them, but he knew today was not that day. Drawing his thoughts together he focused on the crystal in his hand, the map it hung over, and the words of the spell in his mind. Blocking out everyone and everything else in the room, picturing Grace's face, he spoke the words clearly.

The crystal spun over the paper of the map, swinging from side to side. At last, he felt the tug of it in his grasp. When he opened his eyes it stood upright on the map, covering the mountains to the east. He knew it. He had spent nearly a century in the wilderness as a wolf. He knew there was a cave there on the hilltop. He had little doubt it was where he would find Grace.

"Aye, we head out at dusk," he nodded to Seamus and the others, "I know where to find them."

CHAPTER
EIGHT

GRACE ROLLED TO HER SIDE, taking in Rowan's form as he sprawled in the bed next to her. They had taken to sleeping during the day and spending the nights in one another's arms. A table laden with food sat across the cave and she crossed to it. Wondering for the first time, as she looked around the cave, what had possessed her to agree to stay here for so long. No doubt she had been fired and her apartment manager would surely be looking to evict her for lack of payment, as the first of the new month had come and gone.

Sitting down in one of the old-fashioned chairs at the table she began to eat, curling her legs under herself and processing all that she could from her time here with Rowan. So many of her memories had a magical sheen to them, they seemed hazy and confusing. It nagged at her. She didn't understand. Their time together felt as if it had flown by, but in her mind, she had memories of them being together for so much longer than the mere month that had passed.

A noise drew her attention to the man on the bed, the sheets tangled around his legs. The outline of his cock beneath them called to her. She licked her fingers clean and stood, crossing to him. Suddenly she heard it in the distance, the howl of a wolf. It was met by that of another, then another. Her eyes went wide as she wondered what it could mean. Was it Shay and his brothers? The pack of wolves she had met when she reached the Keep the day before Valentine's Day to see Cassidy?

Rowan sat up in the bed and turned to see Grace standing at the mouth of the cave, her back to him. He heard it again, the chorus of the wolves. He knew what it meant, they had found them, they were near. Nearer than he felt comfortable with from the sound of it.

Undoubtedly, they would be here soon. "Grace," he called, and when she turned the questions filling her eyes told him the truth of the matter.

He had slept far too long, he needed to regain his control as it slipped from her mind. His hunting over the past few evenings had proved useless. The townsfolk were scared, and fear kept them locked inside. He hadn't fed in nearly a week, as the exhaustion from it took him over, he allowed himself to doze. Sating his need for Grace, then curling around her body, the two had fallen asleep together. It was past dusk, the moon was high in the sky, and he had not had the chance to hunt before she woke.

"Sweet Grace." He opened his arms to her, summoning her to him.

"The wolves?" she asked as she closed the space between them.

"Aye, we must go." Knowing he wouldn't have time to escape on foot he felt around in his mind to see if he could muster the strength to sift them from this place.

"They're my frie–" The words died on her lips as he shoved himself forward into her mind with no coaxing.

Grace's hands flew to the sides of her face, a sudden headache making the room spin around her. Rowan pushed himself deep into the depths of her inner self, beyond the walls she kept between them while he played in this space previously. Smashing through them in an instant he pushed the thoughts to her. Fear, torture, death. Tears streamed down Grace's face. Her body shook with the pain of having him so abruptly in her mind. The images he fed her of death and destruction at the hands of the wolves made her weep.

"So many women," she gasped. The images of the lifeless bodies of the women Rowan had killed, their chests torn open, hearts gone.

He laced his lies with just enough truth.

"Yes, Grace, we must leave. They're hunting. Searching out their next victim, the women of Kerry are not safe from the wolves." His words reached her ears, but her eyes remained unfeeling as he continued to fill her mind with the lies he wished her to believe.

Something inside her broke when she saw Seamus's face among his brothers'. Centuries of dead women secreted away from the townspeople. Cassidy came to her mind, Olivia, Faith, the poor women who called these beasts husband.

"How?" she gasped as Rowan eased from her mind, giving her the time to absorb all he had shown her. "How have I been so blind?"

Rowan wiped a tear from her cheek. "We must make haste. We must leave this place before they come. I cannot fight them all to protect you. Your heartbeat calls to them, sweet Grace. Come!" he commanded her forward.

Wrapping her in his arms as she took the final step toward him and fell against his chest, he sifted space and time. It was a Fae trick he had never attempted with another. He was unsure if enough of her blood still coursed through his veins for it to work. But try he must. The reprieve they had enjoyed here in the cave was quickly coming to an end and they must seek sanctuary elsewhere.

Grace felt her body pulled apart and then re-materialized. She recognized the feeling. She had been sifted by Fae in the past. Once, before her father had turned on her, she asked him why the Fae called it sifting. She knew in this century it would be more closely related to the idea of teleportation. He told her that it was as if you were sifting sand through your fingers. Time and space, the earth that the Fae were so in tune with each falling through your fingers as a grain of sand would.

When she settled back into herself, she looked into Rowan's eyes. "You sifted us." It came out as an accusation, but she had not intended it as such. She was in awe.

"Aye." Releasing her from his grip Rowan looked around them. This place would do. He had been here before and it was the only place that came to mind as he rushed to get them to safety.

Grace could hear the sound of rushing water, she was sure now it was a waterfall. Looking around she saw they were again in a cave, water dripping from the cracks in the rocks above them.

"Where?" As she looked around, Rowan waved his hand, using the last of the Fae magic he possessed, he transformed the space into a lavish twenty-first century apartment.

"Wicklow." Brushing his hands over Grace's arms he could feel her quivering with what he had little doubt was fear.

"Why?" She wept, she couldn't help herself, the images of what the wolves had done flooded her mind.

"We had to leave Kerry, get beyond the O'Gannigan lands." Rowan lifted Grace, cradling her in his arms as he crossed to the couch.

He had been doing research on this time, he knew she was unaccustomed to the time he was from, and he strived to make her feel more at home this time around.

"There are no wolves here?" Thinking through her question his face fell and Grace sensed his apprehension.

"Aye, there is another pack here in Wicklow. But they do not know of our presence here. The other pack, Seamus, knew you were on their lands. Torin…" he paused, thinking through how much he should tell her. "He followed you to the stones. He saw us leave together. They have been hunting us since." Grace gasped. "You know too much." Her hand flew to her chest as she thought about her encounter with Declan the night she arrived.

Rowan had explored her memories of her time within the Keep enough to know he could use this information to exploit her. He smiled down at her as he kissed her on the top of her head, the fear she felt coursing through her veins awakening the hunter inside him. She smelled like prey. He shook his head. He needed to feed. He had gone far too long without human blood, and he had no desire to put Grace's life at risk if he lost control.

"Shay?" she spoke her friend's name, disbelief filling her mind. He was a killer. "Oh God, Cassidy!" She suddenly feared for her.

"Hush, you've had a fright. You need to rest." Rocking her in his lap as he spoke, he weakly pushed against her mind, he was so exhausted from using the last of his stolen magic and not having fed in too long.

Gently he coaxed her to sleep in her mind as he held her. "Hush now, sweet Grace. You're safe with me."

Carrying her to the bed he laid her down gently and quickly turned to leave the cave. He needed to hunt and feed soon. His desire to feed on her was strong, but he couldn't trust himself to taste her blood and not drain her. He must hunt first, then return before she wakes.

TORIN TOSSED HIS HEAD BACK AND HOWLED TO HIS BROTHERS AS HE caught wind of Grace's scent. They were close. The cave was just over the crest of the next hill. His heart raced. As the five wolves approached the mouth of the cave the scent of blood hit Torin and he let out a low growl. Looking around the space he felt as if he had been transported back in time. It reminded him so much of the seventeen hundreds when he had met Beth and it nearly knocked the wind from his lungs.

There was no sign of them here, shifting, he walked around

the cave. Taking it all in. Grace's cellphone lay on a small table next to the bed, picking it up he slipped it into his pocket. Any hope they had of contacting her this way was now gone. The scent of blood made his nostrils flare and he pulled back the sheet on the bed, it was covered in blood, Fae blood. Grace had been injured from the look of it. He felt his stomach retch and nearly vomited onto the floor. Finding her at last, not only had she been taken from him but, now she was injured, and he had lost the one lead they had.

"Torin?" Seamus called his brother. Torin turned to face him.

All three of his brothers and his father looked on, he knew they could all smell the blood, they could all see it.

"This isn't the end, we will find her," Seamus spoke quietly.

"We just missed them. The bed is still warm," Cormac said and cleared his throat, realizing too late the implications of his words.

"We will return and scry again. They can't have gone far on foot," Brody added.

"How could a bear with a woman on his back have gotten past us in the woods?" Declan was the one who spoke up next. His four sons turned to look at him. "You said the night he took her from the dolmen he shifted into a bear, and she rode astride his back. How did they slip by us? Tis' but one way in and one way out of this cave from the looks of it."

"Aye," Torin confirmed as much, "this is the truth of it. There is no other way out of this cave." He wrinkled his brow in thought. The smell of Fae floating into his mind again. "Can Grace sift?" He turned to Seamus when he asked this.

"No, she is only half Fae," Seamus said and shook his head.

"Do we know what the Dorcha is capable of in this form?" Brody was the one to speak. "We have only ever fought him in another form, one that forced us to banish him. He is now corporeal. We know too little about our enemy and his capabilities."

"Aye, but what we do know is a corporeal body can be

killed once and for all, not just banished." Joy filled Torin at this thought.

All five had spent so many nights searching for Grace and patrolling to keep the town safe that none of them had put much thought into these things before now.

"We need help," Declan declared. "I shall reach out to the McTavish and Roney packs. We have underestimated our enemy, and we will not make the same mistake twice. They need to know the Dorcha has returned. If they have fled Kerry, undoubtedly, he will return to more familiar hunting grounds in Wicklow or Glasgow. The deaths we have seen here will continue. They must be warned. His insatiable hunger will lead us to them."

Torin could hear the truth in his father's words but the hunger he spoke of made him fear more deeply for Grace's life. Would she be his intended victim? It occurred to him then, the blood, her Fae magic.

"Fuck!" He spun back toward the bed, examining it more closely.

"What?" Four heads turned to him.

"He sifted them! He is stealing her Fae magic, using her blood to gain her powers and masking himself with them." Torin's realization meant she wasn't in imminent danger. He would need to keep her alive to continue to feed on her powers. "Perhaps he is weaker in this form? If he is using Fae magic in this way, he motioned around the room. What real power does he possess of his own?"

"Why would Grace allow him to do so?" Seamus knew his friend. He knew her strength and independence. He couldn't fathom it being something Grace would allow.

"Faith," Brody croaked, "you need to speak with Faith."

"Aye?" Torin turned to his brother, the questions in his eyes made Brody nod.

"Compulsion of a sort. Faith can explain," Brody said and made his way from the cave, pulling his phone from his pocket, searching for signal. "Tis' no use up here. We need to return to the Keep."

Torin shook his head, he didn't have time, he needed to continue searching. "There is no time—"

"If he sifted them, there will be no path to follow. They could be anywhere now. We head back to the Keep. You speak with Faith. Da' will contact the other Alphas. We need a plan. We can scry again and perhaps we will know if he went to Wicklow or Glasgow." Seamus's words were rational. Torin knew his brother had a good head on him and that this was the best path to take.

Slowly he nodded. "Aye, I'll speak with Faith in person."

Piling out of the cave, Torin turned and gave it one last look, he could feel her here in this place, she was calling to him. His heart ached. How could he feel for someone he did not know? Was he betraying Beth and his love for her? It was too much, shifting he took off into the woods. He needed to run, he needed to be alone, needed space.

His howl ripped through the night as he made his way into the trees. His brothers and father let him go, he would return to the Keep in due time. But they knew he was struggling, and he needed time to process what they had discovered.

CHAPTER
NINE

TORIN SAT at the table in the great hall listening to Faith's sobs as she told him her story. His bleeding heart felt as if it might shatter in his chest. He knew what Brody and the others had told him from that time. But hearing it from Faith, hearing her words, her sobs, still so affected after so many years had passed.

It told him he was not wrong to still hurt for Beth, if Faith could still have so much pain from what she went through, then his emotions were not strange. As he listened, he learned, the capabilities that he didn't know the Dorcha had, only made him fear more for Grace. The ability to invade her mind, her memories, it could only mean trouble for them.

When Grace was at last returned to them, as he knew she would be, what would be left of her? Faith came home to Brody after two days nearly a shell of a woman, so affected by the torture inflicted upon her in such a short time. Grace had been with the Dorcha for nearly a month at this point. Saving her was his life, he had spent every waking hour searching for her. To come so close today and have them slip through his fingers enraged him.

"We need to find her," he said the words low, under his

breath, he reached for the map and the crystal that lay on top of it.

Torin had made multiple attempts to scry for Grace as soon as he returned to the Keep, all had proved useless. Something was blocking him. He had little doubt the Dorcha, Rowan, he nearly spat as he thought the name, was on to their attempts to track them and would block the magic that had led them to Grace.

"You will find her. You will bring her home," it was Faith's soft voice that drew his attention, she smiled across the table at him, "and no matter what she has been through. You will help her to get through it. She is your mate. It will all be all right in the end."

He wished he had as much faith as she did, but he had loved and lost. He had endured centuries of pain and knew the truth behind heartbreak. If they didn't find her, or if they did and she was too broken to heal. What would it mean for him, for them?

"Thank you, Faith," he told her as he stood from the table and headed across the hall. He was going to search, he needed to put his time to good use and scrying had proved useless.

"Da' said the McTavish and Roney packs are on high alert. If they have any signs of them, they're going to let us know straight away," Cormac told Torin as he passed him. Torin simply nodded, he knew this meant they would have to sit and wait for word from one of the other counties.

Rowan watched the woman walk down the sidewalk through the park, he smiled to himself. They were so foolish, humans, so easy to prey on. He relished the taste of her as he devoured her heart. It had been entirely too long. He was putting Grace in danger by going so long without feeding. But the damned O'Gannigans had kept him from seeking out what he needed so badly.

It didn't matter, they were here now. He would sate his needs this night in Wicklow and if and when the McTavish pack drove them off their lands, he would find another place. His time with Grace had been incredible, the power he took from her was so sweet thrumming through his veins. But he needed a plan to eliminate the packs, he needed to find a way to destroy the wolves once and for all so he and his Grace could rule. He needed to finish his deed and return to the cave, the wards he had put in place would keep them from tracking her once again. However, he feared that as his power waned so would they.

As he licked his paws clean, he thought about how he liked this new form. Living in the shadows for so long in the past had been laborious. Hunting in this form proved easier, and he enjoyed the time he spent in the wilderness. In the past he controlled the beasts in the wild, now he became one. It made him smile. Turning from the lifeless body on the ground before him, he knew he needed to return to Grace. He must feed on her and gather her Fae magic to him before the wolves found them again. Knowing the trail of women he left in his wake this night would draw the McTavish pack to him, he had little hope of remaining here long. Time was of the essence, and he must seek Grace out before the sun rose.

Grace woke, groggy with sleep, and saw Rowan in bed next to her. He was sitting on the side of it, his back to her. She trailed her hand down the muscles of his back, fingertips brushing against his skin. Rowan tensed at first then relaxed into the sensation of having Grace's hands on him. It soothed him, he had never known this feeling before. The joy of having a woman, not to just physically be with her. But to have her support him, be tender with him, it called to something inside him.

"Rowan," she called to him. Rowan looked back at her over his shoulder, she crooked a finger in his direction. Coaxing him to her, she could get used to this life. This magical, wonderful, life. Eternity with him here in the mountains, living off the Fae magic that coursed through the veins of the earth.

Grace smiled as Rowan turned and crawled across the bed to her, a thought flashed in her mind. She realized then, that while this was so enticing and she could live this way forever, they had just run from Seamus and his pack. They were in danger and if they did nothing to eliminate that they would never be free to live the incredible life she had just dreamed. Rowan looked into her eyes. He could see her thoughts roaming there. Knew she was thinking of the dreams he had fed her, danger from the wolves, sanctuary in him. He had spent his time with her when he returned to the cave, coaxing her sleeping mind open to him so he could delve further into it.

Realizing now how pale she was, he wondered absentmindedly if he took too much blood. He needed her Fae magic, but he didn't wish her harm. He would be more careful in the future. Reaching the spot where she sat in the bed with her legs crossed, he kissed her cheek.

"Grace," he purred in her ear as he laid her body back on the bed beneath his. His cravings for her body were growing with each passing day.

"Master," she said and smiled up at him, and he beamed down at her.

"Good girl." She would do anything he asked, and now was the time to put that to the test, Rowan thought. Running his fingers over her cheek, his thumb trailed across her lower lip. "Stand for me," he said as he reached out for her hand and rose from the bed himself. Grace's legs uncurled from beneath her as she followed Rowan from the bed. "Bow," he commanded and pointed to the ground at his feet.

Grace didn't hesitate, she fell to her knees, arms stretched out above her head, she bowed to him, her King, her Master. When he had asked her to do this before she wondered at it, the nagging thought crept back into her mind now in this moment. Why did he need such obedience from her? But as they got into this routine each morning she felt more comfortable with her submission to him. Felt the need to give him this. He was right, she should have done so on first waking but the night before had been an arduous one and it had slipped her mind.

Rowan could see the tension in her body as she knelt. The way she glanced up at him questioningly, he knew Grace was wondering at the gesture. He didn't like it, didn't approve of her not obeying him completely in this. If she couldn't do this without questioning him, when the time came for true decisions to be made and true allegiance to be determined, how would he trust her then? He'd had it under control, then the damned wolves had placed doubt in her mind last night and he could see it there now.

"Rise, Grace." Rowan reached his hand out to her. He was going to teach her a lesson in obedience.

Grace stood, looking at the man before her, placing her hand gently into his. The look in his eyes sent a shiver through her and she was unsure of what was about to happen. Rowan wrapped his arms around her waist and lifted her into his arms. Carrying her to the bed, sitting on the edge of it, he laid her over his lap.

Grace could feel the palm of his hand rubbing small circles over her ass through her jeans. Suddenly, she felt the cool air on her skin, and she knew what he had done. Fae magic, with the wave of a hand her clothes were gone, and she was naked on his lap. The crack of his palm meeting the skin of her ass made her jump. She squeaked out a surprised sound and turned to look up into his eyes.

They were deep, red pools of something she couldn't pinpoint. Fear ripped through her as she stared into them, she couldn't look away, something had her frozen in place. Rowan's hand came down on her ass again, this time when she tried to squirm, she found she was truly locked in place, by magic. This was more than him pinning her to his legs. She was unable to move a muscle, unable to protest. This wasn't the friendly ass smacking he had given her as they fucked in the past.

"Sweet Grace, we have spent enough time together now that I think you should begin to learn the truth," he purred to her as he rubbed circles over the red spot on her ass cheek where he had struck her. "I promise you, I will make you my Queen. We will be happy, but you have been confused about who I am. I'm tired of this game. True obedience is what I desire from you, and I know no other way to instill that than by showing you the power that I am."

Fear. The word crept into her mind. He was saying he knew no other way for her to obey him fully than through fear. Something rubbed against her thoughts, it was dark and oily. Rowan smiled as he worked his way into her memories. He did not coax his way in, nor did he force his way in as he did when they needed to flee Kerry. Instead, he slithered, his shadowy presence crept through her thoughts, her memories, her fears, hopes and dreams. He had access to it all and he was showing her the truth of what he could do.

Grace's eyes glazed over, she felt as if she were ripped out of her body and hovering above it in space. She saw it then, the shadow figure in her mind, curling tendrils around her every desire and fear. Sorting through them, pulling them forward into her mind as it pushed others aside. She couldn't comprehend, didn't understand, it selected memories of her and Rowan together. Playing them for her in her mind like a movie on a screen. It pulled forth images of dead women at the feet of a wolf pack, blood coating their muzzles.

It played in her mind, and fear struck through her like a bolt of lightning at the realization that she was not safe in her own head. The dark shadow swirled around her now, in the room with her as her eyes began to refocus. Rowan was nowhere to be found. His laughter was the only thing she could hear.

He stood over her body, looking down at the woman bound on the bed beneath him as he swirled around the room. While he played in her mind, allowing her to see him this time, he did what he had needed to do from the beginning. Deep gashes on both of Grace's wrists seeped blood, he knew she would be weak, near death he had little doubt, but he needed her magic and her strength. Having fed so recently the blood of the half-Fae mixed with that of the blood of the innocent in his veins and he roared.

He was gaining more strength than he had over the past month, trapped in this corporeal form she had summoned him in. Now, as he swirled around the room in his truest of forms he danced over her pale skin. He snaked himself around her body, he would please her, keep her happily as his pet, his Queen. But she needed to learn, and now it was time.

A memory of his sweet Faith, as she screamed in the tunnels beneath the O'Gannigan Keep filled his mind. The look that was on Abigail's face as he killed her family while she watched and pleaded for her own life. The feel of Hope's heartbeat as he licked the blood from that very heart, looking down into her open chest. The memories of so many women, so many centuries of torture. He had bent them all to his will, all but one, he pushed Gwendolyn from his mind. Refusing to let the rage fill him at the thought of her and Declan O'Gannigan.

It mattered little now in this moment. He need not concern himself with the past. His future was Grace, and she would plead, she would bend, she would scream for him as the others all had. But she would love him. Grace's eyes fluttered open and the shadow in the room sent a shiver through her. She tried to move but found that she was bound. Thick ropes twisted up around her ankles, and thighs, her wrists behind her back were secured to another length of rope around her waist.

"Rowan?" she cried out to him, the darkness in the room keeping her from seeing if he were here with her still.

"Grace," he purred in her ear, she could feel him but still not see him. "Who am I?" he cooed to her, knowing she knew the answer.

Grace was disoriented and confused. She tugged against her bindings. She had done as he asked. She had bowed to him, why was he doing this? How was he doing this?

"I said, who am I?" A whisper of air against her skin, the trailing of the tendrils of shadows down her back tickled her as he spoke.

"Rowan, I—"

"Who the fuck am I!" he roared at her and cut her off, claws sliced down her back and Grace screamed.

"Master," she panted. "Please," she cried.

"Yes." He kissed the side of her face, then she felt it, his tongue trailing over the cuts on her back, lapping at her blood.

Something clicked in her brain, the memory of something. She searched for it in the depths of her mind. Rowan was there, he knew what she was looking for, knew the memory she was trying to recall. He debated for a moment. He could let her see the truth. It mattered little, he would show her now, then bury it in the back of her mind again, replacing it with the false truths he had been feeding her these past weeks.

Rowan slipped deeper into the depths of her memories and found what she was searching for, feeding the images to her. Grace gasped, the first night they were together, clear in her mind now. No longer did she see the shiny magic around the edges of the memory. She saw Rowan, his fangs extending down into her neck as he drained her blood from her. Then as she lay on the bed, lifeless, he toyed with the Fae magic he now possessed.

The truth of him was coming together, piece by piece. He was not Fae as he led her to believe. He was stealing her magic, her blood, and using the power that flowed through her to convince her of these things. Another memory came into her mind, this one much more recent. The moment she locked eyes with him and saw the red gleam in them.

"What are you?" Grace whispered the words weakly.

"Dorcha," he growled to her. The rumble of his chest

pressed against her back reverberated through her. Hands caressed her sides and she moaned loudly. Her mind seeing the truth, her body betraying her to this man, this beast who had so pleased her in the previous days.

Rowan took his time with her then, slowly putting one memory after another from his mind to hers. She would fear him. She should fear him. But as he continued to delve into her mind he wove in the images of them together, through the darkness. Mixing them together, he needed a healthy fear and respect. Just not enough to have her trying to run from him. Gathering the things he had shown her in her mind together he pushed them deeper down, locking them away. Leaving the emotions, they invoked but hiding the truth.

Grace turned and looked around her once more, this time Rowan smiled down at her. She remained bound on the bed, him standing next to it, naked. "Master," she called to him. Rowan nodded and reached for her. As he rolled her onto her stomach, he stroked himself, his fist running up and down the full length of his cock.

"My sweet, Grace," he whispered as he pushed forward into her.

The rope binding her thighs together dug into her skin as he pushed deeper inside her. Filling her with his cock. She tried to squirm. It was useless. Claws grazed over her skin, and she trembled in fear. The memory of them cutting through her back, the feel of them scraping against the bone of her shoulder blades, it was there in her mind.

"Please, Master," she said softly. She wanted to please him, wanted to give him what he desired so he would not hurt her again.

Rowan fucked Grace, pushing her body down into the bed with his own. Claws brushing against her skin, he allowed himself to transform, filling her still. Darkness kissing the tears that rolled down her cheeks. Morphing from one form to another as he took his pleasure from her. Settling into his body once more, he grunted, driving home into her as he filled her with his cum. As he waved his hand the ropes binding Grace disappeared.

Rising from the bed he stood, looking at her, waiting for her to do as he wished. Wanting it to be of her own accord and not because he commanded it. Grace rubbed her wrists, relieved to be free of the ropes. Her eyes met Rowan's, the look in them told her enough. She knew he was expecting something from her, she steadied her breath, slowly rising from the bed.

Impatience grew in his chest as she slowly rose, he wanted to snap his fingers at her, wanted to rage. Grabbing her by the wrist, he jerked her from the bed and shoved her to the floor, his foot pushing down on her back forcing her to bow.

"You may be my Queen, but you will serve me as your King. Starting today, you will learn," Rowan's harsh words filled her mind.

CHAPTER
TEN

THIS IS how things continued between them. Grace struggled to understand the change in Rowan, but she had a new overwhelming fear that if she did not do as he wished she would be in grave danger. He made it clear he wished for her to serve him, to wait on him, to be here when he desired, and be invisible the rest of the time. She learned. It was only a few days since they had arrived in Wicklow from Kerry, but her life was so incredibly different now. The once sweet, doting Rowan was now gone, replaced by the being she called Master.

"Grace?" He called to her as she sat on the couch, thinking about the way things had evolved.

"Master?" She rose and crossed the room to him, falling to her knees at his feet and waiting for his command.

Holding his hand out to Grace, Rowan waited for her to offer him her arm. She lifted it to him, placing her hand into his palm. As he turned it over and exposed the underside of her wrist a claw extended, and he sliced through her sensitive flesh. Grace winced but did not complain. Lips closed over the wound, his tongue hot against her skin. Rowan took his time feeding on her.

He had conditioned her to allow him to do so throughout the day, taking less and more frequently he found he was able to keep her conscious and not risk hurting her. He smiled at her. Grace could see her blood on his lips. She felt numb. Waving his hand over the wound, it healed and he brushed his knuckles over her cheek.

"You need to eat," he told her, waving his hand again, the table he sat at suddenly laden with food.

Grace rose from her knees and sat in the chair beside him. Eating, as she had been told to do, she sat in the silence of the cave and began to wonder at what she was becoming.

"Good girl," he told her, patting her thigh. The praise drew her attention to him again, the look in his eyes telling her he was distracted. Lost in thought, perhaps.

"What is it, Master?" she asked between bites.

"I fear we may have to leave this place." Over the course of the few days they had been here he was beginning to wonder if it was a mistake to come to Wicklow, the pack protecting this land had clearly been tipped off that he had returned. The first night here he fed freely. However, each night after he spent his time evading them as they roamed the woods searching for his trail. "There is danger for us here, the wolves. They are hunting for you."

Rowan pushed gently on the edges of Grace's mind, the images he fed her previously of the wolves and the dead woman. Their escape from Kerry, he used all of it to stoke the fear inside her.

"Master," she gasped, her hand flying to her mouth, "we must leave. Please, I need you to protect me from them. Where can we go?" He thought through her words as she spoke.

Where could they go? He had been using more energy than he wished to use on a protection spell and wards to keep them shielded from magic. He suspected they would be searching for them using their Druid ways, and believed that is how they found them in Kerry. It took an immense amount of time and effort, however, and if he were to get them off pack lands completely, he felt they would be much safer. He would not make the same mistake twice and lead her somewhere that one wolf or another could stumble across them.

"We will leave, on the morrow," he reassured Grace. "I know a place, beyond their boundaries. We will be safe there."

He planned to travel to the Burren, he had come from within the earth, deep beneath the limestone and caves where he rose from the depths. They would return there now. He would take her back to where he had begun his journey. The ancient place would shield them from the wolves' Druid magic. They would be incapable of tracking them there, he would no longer have to exert his energy protecting them and he would be free to hunt without the pack interfering.

The trouble was, the same runes that were carved into the walls of the labyrinth beneath the earth he planned to return to that would protect them, were preventing him from sifting in with the Fae magic he possessed. He could get them close, but they would have to go the rest of the way on foot. Out in the open and unprotected, they would be able to be tracked. Possibly for days as he hiked with her through the underground caves, until they reached their destination. It was a risk, but it was one he would have to take.

Torin was exhausted, the trip to Wicklow was a tedious one and he needed rest. The day that Dale McTavish had called his father to inform him of the three dead woman who had turned up overnight, confirmed that the Dorcha had sought refuge on their lands. The pack left Kerry immediately and made the journey to meet up with the McTavish pack, on their lands.

The next three nights were spent hunting for Rowan and Grace, but always being one step behind them as they roamed the countryside. Their attempts to scry for Grace had turned up nothing, and Torin suspected that Rowan was using more of the Fae magic he was draining from Grace to block them in their search. Rory, Sullivan, and Liam sat at the table in the hall of their Keep, their father Dale at the head of it. Declan to his left, Torin looked around at the familiar faces of his brothers as they listened to the two Alphas speak, planning their next move.

"We've been closing in on him. No doubt we will find them. The women have all turned up around the state park," Dale told Declan.

"They're in the caves under the fall." Torin looked up quickly, unsure who of the McTavish pack had spoken.

"Aye?" he asked, it made sense, they had found them in a cave in Kerry, if he was comfortable in those places, familiar with them, he would continue to return to them now.

"Aye, I suspect it to be true." It was Rory who had spoken. He pulled the map across the table toward him and pointed out the falls, "Here. It is right in the center of where the women have been found. He is hunting out around where he is holed up."

Torin jumped up. "Then we need to go. Do you know it? Know how to navigate it?" he asked Rory as he continued to study the map.

"Sasha does," he told the group of men who turned to look at him as they waited for him to answer Torin's questions.

"No, I won't ask you to bring her into this. It isn't safe. We don't need to put any one in danger unnecessarily." Torin's heart dropped, they would have to go in blind.

"I appreciate that, but it is not what I mean. She can speak with us about it. I was not suggesting she come." The look on Rory's face told Torin he had misunderstood.

Of course, what was he thinking? These men would not be willing to put their mates in harm's way any more than his brothers would. He was fighting to protect a woman he knew to be his mate but knew little else about. The idea that Rory would allow a woman he had spent centuries with to face the Dorcha was absurd. Torin wasn't thinking clearly, he could see that now. He nodded in Rory's direction, the two exchanged a wordless glance between them.

Sasha had shared everything she could recall about the caves under the falls before they headed out to search them. The information she provided them about the entrance to the caverns and the most likely place to find them deep in the belly just under the largest of the falls had proven useful thus far. As Torin kept his nose to the ground, his paw splashing through puddles of water and muck he caught it, the scent of Grace filled his nostrils.

Tossing his head back, he howled, the sound echoed off the stone around him, traveling to the eight other wolves who were tracking their way through the caves. Seamus and Cormac were nearest to him and rushed in his direction. He didn't wait for them, he couldn't, his heart raced. He was so close. He could hear movement in the cave up ahead. See shadows cast on the stone at the end of the tunnel by light. They were here, he had found them.

Torin burst into the cave, his eyes fell on Grace's figure on the bed, Rowan standing next to it. She was naked and bound. Growling low in his chest he stalked toward the Dorcha. Eyes flashed red and a snarl escaped from his lips. Torin lunged toward him, before his claws had the chance to collide with his chest he vanished. Sifting right before his eyes.

Torin shifted, he turned to Grace on the bed, her eyes filled with fear. "It's okay, I'm here. You're safe."

"No!" she screamed. "Please! Don't kill me. I don't want to die! Rowan!" The fact that she was calling to the Dorcha for help was not lost on Torin.

"Grace, we are going to take you home. It's okay. I'm Seamus's brother, Torin. You're safe now." She squirmed on the bed, bound as she was it was useless. Torin's hands reached out for her.

"Don't touch me, you monster! I've seen what you do. The women you and your pack have been feeding on." Confusion filled Torin, but the fear in Grace's eyes as she spoke told him she believed what she said.

He made to touch her again, the second his hands grazed against her skin he felt the magic surge between then, electricity filled the air. He closed his eyes, hesitating a moment, it was true then, she was his mate. The moment of hesitation cost him.

"What was tha—" Grace began, but before she could finish the question the Dorcha sifted in on the opposite side of the bed, his hands reached out, taking hold of her and he sifted her out with him.

One moment Torin's hands were on Grace, the next they fell to the bed, she was gone. "Fuck!" he roared as Seamus and Cormac burst into the cave. "I had her! I had her right here in my arms, and he sifted them again." Torin turned and sat on the edge of the bed, his head in his hands. "She said we were killing these women, feeding on them. She screamed, scared of me." His stomach turned as he said the words out loud. "I touched her. I felt it, the magic between us. She is my mate." Sighing heavily, he stood from the bed and turned to his brothers. "She is my mate. She believes me a monster and would rather be with that... that thing!" he spat the words.

"We will have to find a way to prevent him from sifting her next time. Otherwise, there is no point in us tracking them across the country again and again, for them to just vanish into thin air the moment we arrive," Seamus said as he stepped to Torin's side and rested his hand on his shoulder.

"Or we can beat him at his own game. We need a Fae. A full Fae who can sift in, grab her, and sift out with her." Torin's voice was filled with the confidence he felt in his plan.

"That would be an incredible idea, if we knew a Fae who would be willing to help us. They aren't very fond of us, or of humans for that matter, they're even less fond of Grace. Being that she is a half-blood," Seamus told his brother, not trying to hide the disappointment in his voice.

"We do," Torin said and marched right past Seamus and

Cormac out of the cave. Headed the way he had come, he needed to get out of here. He couldn't stand the smell of Grace mingled with the scent of sex and the Dorcha. It was eating away at his insides.

"Who?" Cormac asked, following close on his heels.

The three brothers encountered the rest of the wolves in the narrow passageway as they left the cave behind. "They're gone," Seamus told them, "Sifted out."

"Torin," Cormac called to Torin as he closed the gap between them, the others having fallen into step behind them.

When they burst into the night air, again leaving the caverns behind them, Torin turned and faced the pack.

"We need to go to the Roneys. We need their help. It is the only way we are going to be able to reach Grace. We can get her from the Dorcha then deal with him. But Seamus is right, no matter how many times we track them down if he continues to simply sift them away as soon as we close in, this will go on for an eternity. We need a Fae who can sift." Torin watched as some of the men in the crowd around him made the connection, understanding dawning on their faces.

"Quinn." Dale McTavish was the one to speak, Torin nodded.

"She can sift in, grab Grace and sift out. It will take her seconds. The Dorcha will never expect us to have a Fae on our side who would be willing to help. He wouldn't have the chance to react." Torin knew this would work. It was the answer they had been searching for.

"Aye, what makes you think that Cian Roney is going to allow you to use his wife in this way?" Rory spoke up, he had been clear in his feelings about allowing Sasha to aid them. It was clear to the others that he felt Cian would feel the same.

"We must save Grace! It does not hurt to ask," Torin puffed his chest as he spoke, he was ready for a fight, if Rory was going to give it to him then so be it.

"It doesn't, but the fact that you are so willing to put other's mates at risk for the sake of your own says a lot about the kind of man you are," Rory said and glared at him.

"You know nothing about the kind of man I am and what I have lost in the past. I will raze worlds to protect her if I must, no matter the cost." With that statement Torin shifted and took off into the woods.

Rory turned to face the remaining members of the O'Gannigan pack as well as his own. "Am I wrong in this? He is foolish to expect us to risk our mates for his."

Seamus turned to face his father, he knew what was driving Torin and knew the others needed to understand the truth of what Torin had faced. Declan nodded his approval. He understood the silent question in Seamus's eyes.

"This is about more than Grace. It is because of Beth, this all comes down to his losing Beth," Seamus told the McTavish men.

"Who is Beth?" Dale stepped forward, his eyes falling on Declan's face as he saw him cast his glance downward, then turning and looking away. Declan approved of telling them the truth, but he couldn't face the look in their eyes when they learned of what he had done.

"Beth was Torin's love. He believed she was his mate. She discovered the truth of what we are. Torin convinced her not to tell anyone, but they were unable to complete the spell. She was not truly his fated mate," Seamus paused, thinking carefully though how much of the truth they actually needed.

"I did what I must to protect the pack," Declan turned as he spoke, "I made sure the secret would be kept. It was a high price to pay. But it was done, and I cannot take that back now."

"You killed her?" Rory stepped toward Declan, he needed to understand.

"Aye, I thought it was my only option at the time," Declan glanced to Dale, the look in his eyes told him he understood the weight of what it meant to be Alpha, to be the one to have to make these types of decisions.

"He has suffered a great loss in his life," Seamus went on, "he will do what he must to ensure she is returned safely. No matter what it costs. We can support him, but you're right, Rory, it is not fair of us to ask these things of you all. Killing the Dorcha once and for all is one thing. Protecting Grace is another. Putting those we love at risk to do just that is not the answer."

"What makes you think after so many centuries that we could truly kill it now?" Dale raised a brow as he stepped forward. This hadn't occurred to him, banish it again, yes. But kill it, they had never succeeded in this before.

Seamus smiled, looking around at the faces of the other men, and explained, "It has a physical form, it is no longer a ghost we are chasing through the shadows. It is a man, a shifter, it will bleed. It can be killed." He was confident in his assessment. He knew Torin had the same realization. "Did none of you think of this? This is our chance to eliminate it from our lands for good. Not banish it for another century or two. This is our time to kill the Dorcha."

"Shite," Cormac and Brody both said under their breath, turning to look at each other. The McTavish men doing the same. None of them could believe they had failed to realize the truth of this before now.

"Even if the Roneys help us get Grace, we have a bigger problem. Faith explained to us about the Dorcha, and it is clear now that it has been doing the same that it did with her, to Grace. Torin says she believes us the killers of these women," Seamus broke the last of the news he had to share to the men.

"Aye, but I was able to reach Faith in her mind through our bond and help her to see the truth, to heal." Brody tried to give them hope.

"Aye, but Torin has not formed that bond with Grace. She does not know he is her mate, they do not have the ability to hear each other's minds," Cormac pointed out, he had experienced it with Olivia. The time they had been together, when she had no memories of being his mate, they did not have this bond or ability. It wasn't until she knew the truth of what he was and felt the truth of being his mate in her heart that they were able to form it between them. "If Grace does not believe she is truly his mate, in her heart, it will matter little as far as that bond goes."

"Which is why I need to get her back as quickly as I can. We cannot allow the Dorcha to further confuse her with its lies." All eyes turned to Torin as he spoke. He hadn't gone far and returning to the clearing where the others stood now, he heard his brothers' words.

"To Glasgow it is then?" Rory spoke up, he had been the loudest voice against this plan from the beginning, he felt it was only fair he was the first to offer his aid, now that he saw the truth of what they must do.

"Aye," Torin nodded, "thank you."

CHAPTER
ELEVEN

GRACE LOOKED AROUND, she remained bound and naked. She shivered in the cool air surrounding them.

"Master," she said, as a tear rolled down her cheek. They had come for her the way he said they would.

"Hush, you're safe. We got away." Rowan settled her onto the ground and waved his hand over her body. His abilities were tested and he needed to restore his stolen magic, sifting the way he had, took almost all that remained.

Grace was released from her bindings, clothes draped over her body once more. She lifted to her knees and looked up into Rowan's face.

"Master, I'm scared. I don't want them to find us again." She stretched, at last being free. She wasn't sure how long she had been bound on the bed this time.

It seemed that the time they spent together was growing less and the time she spent alone, bound and waiting for his return greater.

"We will be safe here," Rowan told her, his hand pressing to the side of her face.

He had sifted them to the Burren, but he needed to get her into the depths of it where they would be protected by the ancient runes that covered the stone walls in the inner chambers. Surveying her face, he debated if she would be well enough to travel on foot or if he should shift and take her on his back. He had no Fae magic left, he felt drained, and he knew the long trek into the depths of the earth would prove exhausting. He needed to feed soon, the pack in Wicklow had been closing in on them and he hadn't been able to feed since the previous day. But the decision to feed on Grace and restore some of his strength was one that could alter the course of their journey and he was unsure.

Grace looked into the eyes of the man standing before her, he studied her closely. She could tell he had something on his mind but was unsure what it was. Thinking it was simply the trials of what they had been through with the wolves finding them she pushed the concern away and tried to focus on what lay ahead.

"Where are we?" she asked him as she took the time to look around and take in her surroundings.

"The Burren, I have a place here for us. A place they will not be able to track us, so they will be unable to find us. We will be safer here than we were before. They were tracking us before, tracking you." Grace's eyes widened at this. The idea that it was her they were following, her they had the power to trace no matter where they went.

"I'm sorry, Master." She felt as if it were her fault. She should have known, should have suspected sooner.

"My sweet Grace, you are not at fault. They are bad people. They will continue to hunt to the ends of the earth. I will keep you safe from them," Rowan consoled her.

"Why? Why me?" She was so confused. She was nothing to them. Seamus had been her friend for so many years. But what was possessing them to hunt her now in this way, she couldn't understand. Fear crept into the edges of her mind. She was trembling with it.

"Hush, no. Do not worry about it. I will end them, we will

be safe here, and I will find a way to end the wolves once and for all." Rowan bent and kissed her on the cheek.

Grace pressed her body against his, wanting to feel him wrap his arms around her. Wanting to be safe in his embrace. His words told her she was safe, she wanted his body to do the same. Suddenly she felt her face flush, her desire for him taking her over. Rubbing herself on his thigh that had slipped between her legs, she moaned.

Rowan knew if they did not make haste they would be out in the open, able to be tracked again. He had a craving for Grace though, for her blood and he wanted to sate his needs now. If they were tracked, he knew they would never make it from Wicklow to the Burren in time to reach them. He had sifted them here and the wolves wouldn't be able to do so. Making the decision he decided there was time.

Running his hands up Grace's sides under the hem of her shirt Rowan let out a low hiss, the thrum of magic he could feel beneath her skin called to him. Her body called to him, he needed her now. Grace slipped her fingers down beneath the waistband of Rowan's pants, seeking him out. Finding him hard and ready for her, she closed her hand around his shaft.

"My sweet, Grace," he purred in her ear as she ran her hand up and down his length in his pants.

"Master," she said and smiled up at him.

Rowan turned Grace in his arms, pressing her forward against the stone wall. Lowering her pants and then his own. He pressed forward into her from behind.

Grace arched her back, her breasts pressed against the stone wall in front of her, Rowan's hands squeezed her ass as he pushed deeper into her heat. Grace could feel him swell inside her, she knew he was taking, not giving in this moment. Sadness filled her. She wanted to please her Master, but she wanted to find her own pleasure in him as well. She craved the first days they were together, the kindness he treated her with, the passion they shared.

While she wanted to please him and be with him the more time they spent together the more he morphed into something else right before her eyes. Distracted by her thoughts, she missed his command of her, an arm snaked around her throat, pulling her body back against Rowan's chest. He growled low in her ear. She had angered him, the fear that had been growing inside her over the past few weeks surged to life inside her. What had she done? Searching her brain for an answer she couldn't find, darkness began to seep into her vision. The blood flow being cut off, her airways blocked.

"Master, please," she barely croaked out the words.

"Sweet Grace, where have you been?" He played in the memories she was thinking of. Toyed with her mind, it displeased him, he wanted her here. Wanted her present in the moment with him.

Claws extending, he drew them down over her arms. Watching the blood drip down over her skin. Grace screamed. It echoed off the walls around them. She could feel Rowan's claws slicing her open, his tongue trailing over the blood. The image flashed into her mind of him, his mouth on her wrist. Rowan dove into the memory, shattering it. He instead fed her images of them together in bed, sweet and loving, the first days they spent together. Grace melted back against him.

"Come for me, sweet Grace." He was still buried inside her. His fingers slipped down over her clit and she bucked back against him.

Grace could feel the tingle of pleasure moving through her body. Filled by Rowan's cock, his fingers on her clit. She moaned, forgetting the pain in her arms where he had torn open her skin. Rowan pulled back from Grace, turning her to face him. He lifted her by the waist, settling her back down over his cock as she wrapped her legs around his waist. Looking into Rowan's eyes as he filled her again Grace tensed, the red gleam in them shooting fear through her.

"Hush," he tried to reassure her as he felt her body shake under his touch.

Time was running short. He did not want to continue to be here out in the open. But she was coming around again, and he must put in the effort to keep her compliant. He did not desire to have her fighting him every step of the way. With his Fae powers waning he would have to resort to brute force over her and that was not in his plans.

If he could sway her mind and body back to him with tenderness now, then perhaps she would relax. His demeanor changed. Grace picked up on it, looking into his eyes she wondered if the red gleam she saw had been a trick of the light. She wiggled herself in his arms, brushing her clit against his pelvic bone as he drove home into her.

"Yes," she cried out.

One after another he fed her memories of their time together, including the ones he had fabricated of them as well. Grace saw them flashing before her eyes happily living together. Ruling over the lands of Ireland, she was his Queen. He was her King, her Master. Fear was replaced with the ecstasy of passion, as the lies he wove into a beautiful story in her mind began to settle.

"Grace, I need to feel you come all over me. I need you now, come for me." His hand grazed the side of her face.

Lifting her from him again and again he used his hands to guide her up and down off him. Groping her ass in his palms as he found his rhythm. The pleasure grew inside her, tinges of it spreading over her body. She chased the feeling, headlong, she dove into it. Embracing the pleasure. As she came apart at the seams she relaxed. Feeling him slide into her more deeply as she relaxed into it.

"There's my girl." Rowan could feel her inner walls tighten around him. She was close and he knew it, "I'm going to fill you with my cum. Come all over me Grace, now."

His hand slid between them, and he pinched her clit, arching her back against the stone wall behind her she let it take her over. The pleasure of being with this man, this beast. As she reached her climax and cried out, Rowan buried his face in her neck, fangs extending out he licked her supple skin. When her blood filled his mouth, he felt the power of it surge into him. Fae magic seeped from Grace into Rowan once more and he glowed internally with it. Her eyes fluttered closed, she grew sleepy, complacent in his arms as he stroked her hair. Coming down from the rush of an orgasm, she relaxed into his arms, letting him cradle her in them.

He took more than he needed, took all that he could and still keep her alive. Grace went limp at last. Rowan lay her gently on the ground and pulled his pants up. As he looked down at the body of the woman at his feet, he wondered how much longer he could keep this up. He couldn't lose her, his need for her power only continued to grow. If he lost her, he would be trapped once more as a shifter and unable to do what he must. The Fae magic in her blood was the only thing that would allow him to reach his goals. Lifting her gently back into his arms he turned and made his way through the maze of tunnels that lay between him and his goal.

The crackle of magic filled the air seconds before they appeared. Rowan didn't have time to react. A woman stood before him, Torin by her side. It was seconds, he was so caught off guard he didn't have time to sift. Grace was there one moment and gone the next. He roared, it bounced off the walls around him.

Torin could hear the sound of Rowan's roar still ringing in his ears as they reappeared in the Roney Keep, the eyes of all three packs' members settling on them. Grace in his arms. The magic that hummed between them everywhere their skin touched told him the truth. Her body was limp, lifeless. He worried they had been too late. But he could hear her gentle heartbeat, it was weak in her chest, but it was there still.

"We need to get her home, to Kerry," he said, looking around at the faces of his brothers as he spoke.

"I can take you," Quinn offered.

"Aye, but we will have to follow on foot. Will you be safe with her alone until we can make the trek?" Declan asked him.

"Aye, I've got her." Torin turned to Seamus.

"How many can you sift at once?" Seamus asked Quinn. "I don't want them entirely unprotected."

"Aye, I can take you three." Quinn looked exhausted as she spoke.

Cian didn't like putting his wife through this. They had pulled it off and retrieved Grace from the Dorcha, but she was heavily pregnant and using her powers was wearing her down after so many years of living as a human amongst wolves.

"Take them to the O'Gannigan Keep and come straight back," Cian told Quinn as he brushed his hand down her long white hair.

She nodded, then in the blink of an eye, she, Torin, Grace, and Seamus were gone.

Torin took Grace to his apartment. He felt he could breathe easy. The Keep was protected from the Dorcha entering. Regardless if he was able to sift again he would not be able to enter these walls and reach Grace.

"I should stay?" Quinn asked, following Torin up the stairs. "She is going to need a friendly face." She shrugged.

Seamus tilted his head to the side and asked, "You know Grace?" He had wondered at her decision to help them without a second thought. It was obvious. Torin didn't question it at the time, but Seamus felt that there was more to the story.

"Aye, she and I go back." Quinn didn't elaborate.

The Fae were naturally secretive, Seamus knew this, especially from the time he had helped Grace with her father. But he didn't know much about Quinn and this new information meant he knew less about Grace than he thought.

"If you think it will help." Torin lay Grace down on the bed and turned to Quinn. "She was terrified of me back in Wicklow. If she has friends she trusts when she wakes I think it would be helpful." He turned to Seamus and asked, "Can you get Cassidy as well?"

"Aye," Seamus replied and left the room, heading to find his wife.

"Perhaps you should leave," Quinn said as she settled into a chair by the bed and glanced at Torin. "I can talk to her, explain the truth." Torin hated the idea, he didn't want to be away from Grace, but he knew Quinn was right. Reluctantly he shifted from foot to foot, nodding at last and leaving the room.

Grace moaned, her body ached, and she felt as if she were weighted down. As her eyes fluttered open she looked around. Her unfamiliar surroundings startled her. A hand rested on her arm. Long feminine fingers met her eyes. Following the trail of her arm to her face her eyes rested on Quinn's face. She graced her with a smile.

"Hey, you're safe now," Quinn brushed her fingers over Grace's cheek.

"I'm so tired," images flashed into her mind and panic began to fill her, "where are we? Where is Rowan?" Trying to sit up she heard another voice and glanced around the room.

"Lie back down, it's okay. We can explain," said Cassidy. Grace saw her friend and fear coursed through her.

"The wolves!" she screamed. "They're killing women. Feeding on them, Cassidy. You're not safe. Where are we? We need to go. We need to find Rowan."

"Grace," Quinn said and waved her hand over her friend, she needed her to see the truth. But her Fae magic could only do so much, her mind had been filled with lies and deception. Grace felt a calm move over her, the soothing feeling of magic wrapping around her. She could feel the magic enrobe her and she looked to Quinn, confused as to why her friend was doing this to her.

"Quinn?" she said, it was barely audible.

"We need to speak. You need to hear some things. Things

that are going to be hard for you to understand." Quinn pressed her hand to Grace's arm, infusing her with more calm.

Cassidy came and knelt next to the edge of the bed at Quinn's side.

"Your spell," Cassidy started, "the night in the dolmen. Grace, it…" she paused, looking for the right words, "it went wrong. It worked, at first. But then something intervened. Something dark, it used the magic you called forth for its own advantage."

"Rowan? It worked, he came to me, I summoned him." Grace's voice cracked, she was remembering the night in the circle of stones, the words she said, the things she felt. Seeing Rowan for the first time, the magic she had felt, told her that her mate was there. "The magic. It told me the truth. My mate came."

"Aye," Quinn nodded, "your mate was there. He is not who you left with." She didn't wish to mince her words, or lead her on any longer. "The Dorcha—"

"Dorcha!" Grace had heard the name, fear filled her veins and she tried to sit up on the bed again, Cassidy urged her to lie back down. "I know that name." She searched her mind, the memories she had felt hazy, she could see the magic around their edges. "He showed me, I saw the being." Confusion filled her voice.

"Let us tell you a story. An ancient one," Quinn said and held her hand, patting the back of it, still soothing her with her magic.

Cassidy pulled a thick tome from the foot of the bed and lay it in Grace's lap, pulling the cover open as Grace looked down on the old pages inside. The three women sat in silence as Grace read the ancient words on each page, taking her time, sorting through what she thought she knew to be the truth. It occurred to her that the memories that had the magic shimmer to them were the ones that this tome proved to be lies.

"But I have memories, things I've seen," she said and shook her head trying to make sense of it.

"Faith can explain those, she has the same," Cassidy spoke softly.

"Faith? Brody's wife?" Grace remembered meeting her, spending time with her and Cassidy the day she had arrived in Kerry. "How is Faith involved?"

"Keep reading," Quinn urged her to return to the book in her lap.

Grace turned the page, gasping as she read over the words there. The story of how Faith had been taken by the Dorcha. How the wolves banished it into the earth, in the dolmen.

"Dear Gods, what have I done? What have I invoked?" Grace felt tears prick the corners of her eyes, the hot moisture spilling down her cheeks. "I've doomed us all. For centuries this beast tormented the country, and I released it back onto us. Those women are dead because of what I've done." She wept, falling forward into Quinn's arms.

Quinn rubbed her back gently and said, "Hush, Grace. You did not doom us. You were fooled, just as so many have been fooled by evil in the past."

"I am a fool," she wailed, "to think it love. Fate," she snorted out the word, "what a fool I've made of myself." Pausing, she looked between the faces of her friends. Something occurred to her, something they had said, something she had felt. "But he was there? At first, my mate?"

"Aye, I was," Torin had crept into the room silently. He had been listening at the door, waiting for the right moment. He couldn't wait any longer, he needed to see Grace. Needed to see she was awake and well.

"Who?" Grace jerked back the moment she placed him in her mind, the man who had come to the cave, the wolf. "You killed…" She trailed off, seeing the magic slashed through the memory. "No, it's not true?" Looking around at the faces of the other three in the room with her they all shook their heads.

"It's not, we did not kill them. We have been protecting them for centuries," Torin said and took a hesitant step toward Grace. She flinched, her mind telling her one thing, her heart another. He paused, not wishing to cause her any discomfort.

Pressing her fingers to her temples she squeezed her eyes closed and tried to sort out what her mind was telling her. As she opened her eyes, they crossed over the face of the man standing by the door. He looked so much like Seamus. She knew he must be his brother. Not Brody or Cormac, his name came to her mind at last.

"Torin?" she asked, still trying to piece things together.

"Aye," he nodded, taking another small step toward her. "I followed you, seeing you leave the Keep. I was there, in the dolmen. What you felt, the magic," he paused, Quinn and Cassidy stood and stepped from the edge of the bed. "It called to me, too."

Torin took the now empty seat next to the bed. He held his hand out to Grace. Not taking hers but offering his, if she chose to make the move and close the space between them. Grace looked up at Quinn and Cassidy, both nodded, smiles on their faces. They both knew what she would feel, what the experience would be like the moment she touched Torin's hand. Hesitantly she placed her palm into his open one, lying on the edge of the bed. Grace could feel it instantly, the buzz of magic shocked her, almost electrical, up through her arm. Torin's broad smile reached his eyes as they met hers, filled with shock.

"Hello, Grace, 'tis nice to meet you, at last. I have waited so many centuries to find you." His words fell around her heart, the magic she felt in the dolmen just before Rowan had appeared mirrored what she felt now.

"Torin?" A tear slipped down her cheek and as he raised his hand to brush it away, almost as if they had completed a circuit, she saw the magic fill the air around them.

Swirls of blue, yellow, and green shimmered before her eyes. Cassidy and Quinn took their cue, as Cassidy made her way to the door Quinn sifted herself home. Torin and Grace sat in silence. She watched the magic in the air around them.

Feeling breathless she sighed and said, "Torin."

His name sounded so sweet on her lips. His heart ached for the past, but so deeply he craved what he could see in his future. Beth was his past, he had hurt for so long over her loss, but it was time to let her go. Time to take this step forward into the future and what it held for him. At last he saw the truth of it, this was not a betrayal of Beth. She would not have wished him to live for an eternity alone and in pain. Leaning forward, as he cupped Grace's cheek in his hand, he felt her shift on the bed, meeting him halfway there.

As Grace felt her lips brush against Torin's, the explosion of magic filled the air around them. She gasped, it felt so incredible, so strong, so right. As Torin slipped his tongue between Grace's lips, opening her mouth to him, his hand slipped into her hair pulling her closer to him, allowing him to deepen the kiss. Grace winced in pain as Torin leaned forward on the edge of the bed, the cuts down the backs of her arms stung when he brushed against them.

Pulling back from her he looked down and saw the pain in her eyes. "Are you all right?"

"My arms and back ache," she told him, unsure why she had been in so much pain since she woke.

"Roll onto your side," Torin said and stood, coaxing Grace onto her side so he could see her back.

Lifting her shirt gently he revealed claw marks over her skin, dozens, all in different stages of healing. He knew from the scent of her blood in the caves he had found her in, had seen the blood on her sheets, saw the Fae magic the Dorcha had possessed, it all made sense. All the pieces fell into place, but Grace clearly did not know. As if seeing her body for the first time she looked down at her wrists, both had deep gashes across them, some healed, some perhaps only a day old. She remembered the pain in the backs of her arms as she screamed while Rowan held her pinned to the wall in cave. The images he had shown her of him, her wrist to his mouth.

"Torin?" She looked back over her shoulder at him as he studied her back. "I don't understand. I have memories, but they're hazy, fogged over."

"Your blood, your Fae magic, he was stealing it from you," Torin explained and helped Grace to roll back onto her back. "It's okay. You're safe here in the Keep. There are wards, he can't cross them."

Grace nodded slowly. Exhaustion was taking her over. Yawning, she leaned into Torin as he moved from the chair to the edge of the bed. She wanted to feel him close, wanted to feel the magic between them. It thrummed beneath her skin, making her feel alive.

"You can rest, I've got you." Leaning down he kissed her on the top of her head. "Sleep Grace. It's okay. Sleep."

He wouldn't leave her side. He refused to leave her unprotected. Understanding dawning on him about Seamus and Cassidy. The things his brother had done last year once baffled him, but it all made sense now.

CHAPTER
TWELVE

A KNOCK on the door roused them hours later. Seamus opened it a crack and motioned for Torin.

"I'll be right back," Torin told Grace as she looked at him questioningly.

She nodded, stretched, and rolled onto her side as Torin left the room. She was deep in thought about something, she needed to speak with him. But it could wait. She knew the Dorcha was still a threat to them all and he must aid the pack in their attempts to find him.

"They're back," Seamus told Torin as soon as the bedroom door was closed behind him. "Da' wants to head to the Burren at nightfall to hunt him. The McTavish and Roney packs are coming. This is our chance. He is at last in a form that we can eliminate."

"I can't leave her," Torin said and shook his head, "I must stay."

"She will be safe in the Keep. You must come. Da' won't hear of you staying behind," Seamus told his brother. He knew the truth of it, though, and continued, "If you don't come, you'll regret it. You might not see it yet, but I can see it in your eyes. Your desire for revenge, it will eat away at you if you choose not to come."

Torin .thought through what Seamus was telling him, sighing, he accepted the truth. "Aye, I'll be ready." He patted his brother's shoulder, then turned and headed back into the room. Back to his Grace.

Before the door was completely closed, she had the question out, "Who's Beth?" Torin froze, his hand still on the doorknob, his heart felt like it shattered. He turned to look at Grace, her face covered in questions. "You called to her in your sleep," she said and scooted toward the edge of the bed.

"Aye?" he said and cleared his throat, feeling guilty again.

Not because he felt he had done something wrong to Beth, but because he felt that he was now betraying Grace and she was put in this position.

"She is someone from my past, centuries ago," he replied, his voice was low. Grace could hear the hesitation in it.

"You loved her very much," she told him, she didn't need to ask she could feel it in her heart.

"Aye, but she was not my mate." He stepped to the edge of the bed and sat down.

Opening his arms to Grace, she leaned forward into his embrace. The magic she felt when he closed his arms around her made her smile.

"She died?" Grace knew she was right, if she was not his mate she would have aged and died, not lived more than her mortal life on this earth.

"Aye, she was killed…" Torin paused, he knew the truth would come out. It always had a way of doing so. "She found out about us. She was killed by my father."

Grace gasped, her hand flying to her mouth. The memories from the day she meant Declan O'Gannigan coming to her mind. The tone he had addressed her with, the tension she had felt in the room of wolves, the realization she had made about them and what they truly were.

"To keep your secret?" She didn't need to ask. She knew the truth of it in her heart.

"Aye, he thought it was the right thing," Torin said and sighed.

"You've forgiven him?" Grace shifted, she wanted to see Torin's face.

"I tolerate his existence," he bit out the words, "I hated him for letting you live the day you discovered the truth. But I understood, you are not a human, and thus different rules applied. He says he has grown to believe differently than he did so long ago." Torin shrugged.

"You don't believe him?" Grace reached her hand out for Torin's. She wanted more skin to skin contact between them.

"I believe he has regrets, but I do not believe he is truly accepting of his role in what happened." Torin brushed Grace's hair behind her ear. Kissing her on the cheek.

"You're leaving?" Grace at last decided to change the topic.

She had heard Seamus and Torin speaking in the hall on the other side of the door. They were going to leave and find the Dorcha.

"He is in the Burren," she told him, it had slipped her mind previously.

"Aye, it is where we scryed for you. We are going back for him. In this form, Rowan can be killed this time. We have banished him many times before, it always claws its way back. The form you summoned forth can die once and for all." Torin was secure in the belief that they could kill the Dorcha this time once and for all.

"Aye, I want to help," she said and scooted closer to Torin, letting him hug her tightly to his chest.

"No, you'll be safe here." She bristled at the tone he used. It reminded her of something, a memory flashed into her mind of her bowing for Rowan.

"I'll not be told what to do." Torin laughed at her outburst.

"Aye, ye' will. Ye' wee Fae. A mighty heart you have," Torin said and kissed her again.

"Do not mock me!" She hated being half-Fae. She so wished

she had the full power of a Fae at her fingertips, she would show him now, if only she had the strength.

Smiling, she remembered one of the tricks she had been taught in the past, she snapped her fingers and in a puff of smoke she disappeared. Torin's eyes went wide, for a minute he thought she had sifted out of the room. But he could still feel her in his arms, still smell her.

"Mmm, glamor?" He pulled her against him even though he couldn't see her.

"Aye." She dropped the glamor and reappeared in front of him. It was her biggest party trick. "You didn't buy it?"

"I could still feel you," he said and tickled her sides, teasing her. "You're going to have to do better than that to impress me, wee fairy."

Grace turned red and said, "Do not call me a fairy."

Torin burst into laughter, if she had been standing, he was sure she would have stomped her foot at him.

He pushed her backward onto the bed, kissing her neck as he did. "I've caught myself a wee fairy!" he whispered in her ear.

"Fuck you!" Grace growled at him.

"Mmm, 'tis the plan," Torin replied and slipped his hand beneath Grace's shirt.

She arched her back and moaned as his fingers grazed over her skin, pushing her bra aside he kneaded her breasts in his hands. Grace wrapped her legs around his waist and ground herself on him, she could feel his arousal and she wanted to have him fill her now. She wanted him to block out the memories of Rowan, of the things he had done to her, the things she had done for him. She needed to know the truth of what it was like to be with her mate and erase the lies he had told her.

"Grace?" Torin paused as he kissed her earlobe. "We can slow down. I know we've just met. I do not mean to rush you into anything." Her heart squelched in her chest, as he told her this. He would not force or coerce her in any way. He wanted her to be fully his. She smiled at the thought.

"Please, Torin. Show me what it means to be your mate." She pressed her lips to his and the magic began to fill the room around them.

A thought occurred to him, he wanted to try something, but he knew they needed to at least start the druid ceremony between them for it to work. Sitting back on his heels on the bed he started to speak the words, looking down into Grace's eyes as he did. She could understand parts of what Torin was saying, she had worked in the library at Trinity college for long enough and was old enough to understand Gaelic. She gathered the majority of what he was saying, though admittedly some of it was lost on her. The last line, however, she fully understood.

"*Beidh grá agam duit i gcónai,*" Torin finished his part of the spell, smiling down at Grace. She needed only repeat the final line back to him and it would be done. They would be bound for eternity as mates.

"Always?" she asked, knowing the translation of his final words, *I will always love you.* She wanted confirmation that this wasn't just an empty promise. She had been alone for so long. She had made so many mistakes in her journey for love.

"Always," Torin nodded and bent to kiss her. "When you're ready. The spell will be completed, you only need repeat it back to me." Pressing his lips against hers he began to explore her body with his hands once more.

Torin slipped his hands over Grace's hips. Hooking his fingers beneath the waistband of her jeans, pulling them down. He took his time, taking in every inch of her perfect body as he revealed it. It had been so long since he'd had a woman. He had waited, never expecting the day to come. Completely taken off guard by the fact that the day had come at last.

"Grace," he said and kissed her hips, trailing his fingertips over her thighs, he followed their path with his lips. Kissing the insides of her thighs, down to the bend of her knee and back up to the sweet spot between her legs. The thin piece of fabric that separated them was too much, he needed it out of the way. Grace lifted her ass off the bed as he tugged her panties, pulling them down and tossing them across the room behind him.

"Torin, please," Grace said and squirmed, his eyes roamed over her body. She wanted his hands on her again, wanted to feel the magic of his touch. The heat of his skin, all of it, she needed more of it.

Bending over her again he slowly began peppering her with kisses, her hips, and down her thighs once more. When he slipped his fingers up and down her slit, she moaned and arched her back, urging him into her.

"Please," she pleaded with him. His mouth closed over her, his hot tongue lapped at her clit. "Yes!" she gasped out.

Grace grabbed the hem of her shirt and awkwardly pulled it off over her head as Torin leaned back and looked at her, interrupted from what he had been doing by her movements. She pulled her bra off with as much haste as she had her shirt. Torin's laugh filled her ears, it was carefree, and she smiled down at him as he settled between her thighs again.

"Eager little thing, aren't you?" He teased her, "A very impatient wee fairy." He smiled as he buried his tongue inside her pussy.

Grace didn't have the chance to protest or scold him for calling her a fairy again, she twisted her fingers in the sheets. Pleasure flowing through her, the mix of the magical feeling moving under her skin from where he touched her combined with the toe-curling pleasure he was giving her had her flying. She felt like she was looking down at her body from above, an observer of the ecstasy she was feeling.

Torin couldn't get enough of her, he wanted to please her, to make her come again and again, until she was putty in his hands. *Grace*, he called to her in his mind, her body jerked. Grace sat up in bed. Eyes wide she stared down at Torin, his mouth still pressed to her pussy, she looked into his eyes, he raised his eyebrows and winked at her. *Tell me what you want sweet wee fairy.*

"How?" she panted out the word, he didn't let up the pressure of his tongue on her clit as she spoke.

Mates. It was all he needed to say, all she needed to understand.

"I want your cock buried inside me." She didn't hesitate. She knew what she wanted in this moment, and she was all in.

Torin's laughter filled her mind. *Like I said, impatient. You can do it, too.* He winked at her again as she settled back on the bed still looking down into his eyes.

Torin? She tried cautiously at first.

Aye, my wee fairy. He purred at her.

Stop calling me that. She was disgruntled. But she couldn't find the strength to care what he called her as he slipped his fingers inside her and stroked her walls.

I'll call you what I like, Grace. You belong to me. He found the sweet spot he was searching for, crooking his fingers inside her he continued to stroke her as he circled his tongue around her clit. *Come for me.*

Grace couldn't get over the fact that he was in her head while he had his mouth on her. It was incredibly intimate, and she loved every second of it. The magic had grown thick in the room around them. She was unable to fathom how she had thought what she had with Rowan had been real, the truth of this moment with Torin showed her how wrong she had been.

Torin growled, the sound reverberated through her, and she raised an eyebrow. *Mine,* he growled at her in her mind. *Stop thinking about him.*

You can hear my thoughts now? She was aghast, not happy that she didn't have privacy in her own mind. Torin could still smell him on her skin and now he was in her thoughts, he needed to snuff out all memories of him. Needed to erase him from her past and claim her as his own.

If they're loud, they come through. Who do you belong to, Grace?

He sucked at her then, nipping her with his teeth, she let out a small squeal.

You, Torin.

She felt it in her heart, she couldn't deny the magic. The feelings she had in this moment for this man. It so mirrored what she felt the night in the dolmen when she called her mate forth. He told her he had been there. It was him she had felt. It was this connection she had so long craved.

Come for me, wee fairy. Stop thinking so damn much! Let me make you fly.

Grace squeezed her eyes closed at his command and tried to relax, she tried to quiet everything that was rushing through her mind, tried to just be with him in this moment. It was no use, Rowan's face, the images of them together filled her mind again. She couldn't stop comparing these two men. Torin sighed, he wanted to try something. Brody had told him about what he had done with Faith when she had come back from her days in the tunnels beneath the Keep with the Dorcha. He pulled the memory of Grace in the dolmen forward into his mind. The way she looked with the moonlight on her hair, the way she glowed in the night when she called her Fae magic forth. He pushed the memory across their bond to her.

Grace gasped, the sight of herself in his eyes, how beautiful she looked. The emotions she felt in the moment. All of it filled her mind. *Torin.* She whispered to him in her mind. This was a gift, it felt so different from the memories that she had from Rowan, the Dorcha, she corrected her own thought. Those felt wrong, intrusive, this was given to her, not forced onto her.

Grace, let me in. Relax, trust me. Be present with me. Here. Now. He pled with her as he pulled another memory into his mind, them here in his room. Kissing, the magic filling the air around them. The way she looked to him. She was the most beautiful woman he had ever seen. In that moment he knew for certain, there was no doubt in his mind she was his mate. He infused the feelings he had felt into the memory as he pushed it forward to her. She gasped. Her heart felt so full. So incredibly complete.

A tear slipped down her cheek and his thumb quickly brushed it away, he had stopped what he was doing. Leaning on his elbows between her thighs he looked up at her. When she looked down, the reverence she saw in his eyes made her want to weep.

Always? she asked the question, thinking back to the final words of the spell he had spoken.

Always, he promised her.

"Beidh grá agam duit i gcónai," she spoke the words without hesitation. He told her it was all she needed to do to complete the spell. This moment, the feelings she had in her heart. The magic she felt in her heart burst forth from her, the room swirled with the blue, yellow, and green swirls.

Torin moved up over Grace's body on the bed, he needed to hold her, needed to feel her lips on his. Bending down he pressed a kiss to her lips, Grace lifted her mouth to his, twisting her tongue with Torin's. A moan escaped her as he brushed the head of his cock against her clit. Torin wanted to take her, mark her as his.

"I will always love you," he swore to her with his whole heart.

Reaching down between them he took hold of the base of his cock and guided himself into her waiting pussy. Grace arched her back, coaxing him in deeper. Torin's guttural moan filled the room. The magic, heavy in the air around them, came to life again. Grace opened her eyes and looked into his, there was an intense look in them, something she couldn't explain. Torin was fighting it, fighting the shift. This had been his undoing with Beth. He couldn't control himself. He shook his head, clearing his mind.

Hey, look at me. What's wrong? Grace pushed the question into his mind. Knowing even if she tried, he wouldn't have heard her speak the words in this moment.

Torin shook his head again, still trying to clear his mind. Grace wanted to help. She knew he had shown her his memories of her. She wondered if she could do the same, pushing them forward into her mind. The moment they first touched, the magic she felt between them. Their first kiss and the way it made her heart feel. Torin began to relax as he held himself above her. Suddenly she saw it, a young woman lay frightened on a bed and a wolf snarled at her from the foot of it.

He had lost his control in the past, and fear of doing the same had nearly crippled him when he felt the urge to shift this time around.

You're in control of yourself. I trust you, Torin. Placing both hands on the sides of his face as she spoke to him through their bond, she smiled up at him. *Now fuck me!*

She growled the last words at him, letting her impatience show. Torin immediately relaxed and smiled down at Grace.

Such a sassy little fairy!

As he drove forward into her, she cried out in surprise at his sudden movement, unable to protest at being called a name again. Grace wrapped her legs around Torin's waist holding him to her as she ground her clit against him.

I'm going to come. She nearly screamed the words in her mind.

He had gotten her so close as he teased her with his mouth before, that now all it took was the brush of his fingertips over her clit and she came unglued. As she writhed on the bed beneath Torin, he could feel her inner walls clamp down around him. He wanted nothing more than to wash away the Dorcha's scent still clinging to her skin. The urge to make this last was stronger though and he took hold of her ankles, unwrapping her legs from around his waist.

Settling himself between her legs again he trailed his tongue up her soaking slit. *You taste so incredible.* He told her in her mind. Devouring her as his fingers slipped inside and coaxed her toward the edge of another orgasm. *I want you screaming for me.* Torin winked at her as he continued his work on her body. Hands snaked up over her abdomen to her breasts and he twisted her nipples between his fingers.

Yes! Grace hissed out her pleasure, it was what she needed. The pleasure pain of his rough hands on her.

Mmm, you want it hard and rough? he purred in her mind as he grazed her clit with his teeth, nipping at her. Then she lifted her ass off the bed and pushed herself harder against his mouth.

Yes, please, Torin.

A memory flashed into her mind, and she tensed. The image of Rowan standing over her demanding she call him Master. Torin flinched. He saw it in her mind through their bond. She hadn't intended to push the images through to him, but nevertheless they were there. Torin tensed, it all seemed like it kept going wrong between them. Each time they tried to get closer to each other the memory of the Dorcha wedged itself back between them.

Grace interpreted the tension in his body, feeling awful for what she had done. She didn't mean to keep pulling Rowan back into bed with them. But her mind was so saturated with him, his memories, her memories of their time together.

Tears slipped down her cheeks. "I'm so sorry," she wept.

Torin rolled to his side, cradling Grace in his arms. This was too much too soon, she needed time to heal. To process what she had been through. He didn't want to mistreat her and force anything onto her. He knew he had rushed the spell, now this.

Hush, get some sleep. It's okay. I'm here. Just let me hold you. He soothed her.

Grace relaxed into Torin's arms, letting him hold her. Her breathing began to change, and he knew she had fallen asleep at last. Torin wrapped his arms tighter around her, refusing to let her go.

CHAPTER
THIRTEEN

ROWAN STOOD IN THE CAVE, examining the runes carved into the walls around him. He knew it would keep the wolves from sifting in again. Since, clearly, they had Fae in their back pockets that he was unaware of. He needed to get to Grace, needed to replenish the power he had been draining from her. Without it, he was nothing but a mere shifter and it grated on him. It had been gnawing on his nerves since the night she brought him back.

The lust he had felt at first, the joy at being able to experience things in this form, quickly faded and left him with the realization that he was less. Less than he had once been. He needed a plan, being off the packs' lands now he was free to hunt, free to reign, but the Fae magic that slipped through his fingers left him craving more.

Not only did he need to get Grace back and regain control over her, but he needed to end the wolves once and for all. For centuries they had blocked him, time and time again, from his goal of supremacy. He would have none of it this time. With enough magic left he knew he could get to Kerry, to the O'Gannigan Keep. But would he be able to reach her, if they had her secured inside the walls there was no hope.

With the bond he had made with her mind, he might be able

to reach her still, draw her out to him. Have her bowing at his feet once more and providing him with the lifeblood of the Fae that he needed in order to bring his plan to fruition. The air around him crackled and hissed. He jerked and saw her form for the briefest of moments. The Fae who had been here before and taken his Grace. Then she was gone, the runes blocking her from sifting in.

They knew where he was. They were making attempts to get in, he couldn't stay. He needed to return to Kerry and secure Grace.

QUINN STUMBLED AND FELL TO HER KNEES, HISSING AS SHE DID. The pain of the runes made her skin burn.

"I can't get to him," she told the men standing around her in a circle. Dropping Declan and Colin's hand, she had been trying to sift in with them.

Cian stepped forward toward his wife. "That's enough now, you're done. You did what you could. I'm not having you involved any longer." Quinn nodded. She knew in her condition she couldn't push the matter any further.

"I'm going to Grace," she told her husband and the rest of the group. Cian nodded and she blinked out of existence.

There was a soft knock on the door and Grace rolled onto her side. Torin's face was so serene as he slept next to her. She slipped from under the covers and headed to see who was there. Quinn stood in the hall of the apartment when Grace opened the bedroom door.

"Hey," Grace reached out for her friend and the two women hugged. "I owe you a big thank you."

"Come, we need to talk," Quinn laced her fingers with Grace's and led her down the hall to the kitchen.

"Coffee?" Grace looked down at Quinn's rounded belly. "Tea?"

"Aye, please," Quinn settled herself onto a stool.

"I want you to come home with me, Grace. I know you have so much untapped power that you can use, and I want to teach you." Grace's jaw nearly hit the floor.

She had wanted a Fae to teach her for so long and had been turned down in the past again and again. The fact that Quinn was offering this to her now was a dream come true. She processed Quinn's request to go home with her to Glasgow as she set the pot of coffee brewing and put the kettle on for the tea. She didn't want to leave Torin, but she wanted this so badly.

"Can Torin come?" She turned to Quinn as she pulled the tea box from the cabinet. Setting it in front of her so she could select her brew.

"Aye, if he wants to. I see no problem with it. Though I suspected he might want to travel to the Burren with the packs." Quinn's words made Grace's heart ache. She didn't want him to leave her.

"Aye, he may. I hadn't considered that," she said as her eyes glanced over to the bedroom door at the end of the hall where Torin still slept.

"Quinn, why now?" It was nagging her in the back of her mind that Quinn was offering this now when she hadn't ever in the past.

Quinn sighed. She didn't have a real answer to the question. She simply felt she needed to do this, where she had never had the strong inclination before.

"It is time. I don't know why. I just feel that you deserve to have someone show you what you're capable of. It isn't fair that your family turned their backs on you and left you to live amongst humans. An immortal alone in this world. I don't know if it is the bond of knowing we are connected in an even deeper way now that we are both fated to live with a wolf for a mate. I truly don't have an answer for you. But I want to do this for you, Grace, please let me."

"The answer is, of course, yes." Grace poured her cup of coffee and handed Quinn her mug for her tea then made her way to the stool next to her and sat.

The two sat in comfortable silence as several moments passed. Both turned to see Torin coming down the hall when they heard the click of the door opening.

"Good morning, ladies," he said and took a step toward Grace and kissed her on the cheek. Then went to pour his own cup of coffee and asked, "What did I miss?"

The looks on their faces told him both were deep in thought.

"I can't sift into the Burren to the Dorcha. We tried, there are runes blocking me," Quinn said.

This was the first Grace was hearing of it and she turned to Quinn. "You didn't tell me that," Grace accused.

"It's not relevant, it isn't an option, so we need to come up with another plan," Quinn voiced her opinion.

"If it isn't relevant then why is it the first thing you tell him?" Grace bristled.

"He knew we were trying. I was just updating him on the failed plan," Quinn replied and shrugged.

It's fine. We will find another way, Torin reassured Grace, he could feel her unease about the fact that they had failed in this and wanted to ease her mind.

Grace nodded. Quinn watched the two, knowing they were having a private exchange. It made her wish she were home with Cian.

"Think about it?" Quinn turned to Grace, "You're both welcome." She smiled and in the blink of an eye she was gone.

"What are you thinking about?" Torin took the now empty stool next to Grace.

"Going to Glasgow and training with Quinn." She knew her decision already. But was unsure if he would approve and come with her. "Will you come with me?"

"I'd follow you to the edge of the earth, Grace. If this is what you want, of course we will go." His hand grazed hers and she felt the magic between them roar to life.

She knew he was disappointed in the way things had transpired between them the night before and she wanted to make it right. Wanted to be with him, needed him to block out the memories she had of Rowan. Torin noticeably flinched.

"Sorry, my thoughts are loud again, I know." She trailed her hand up his arm, wanting to feel the contact between them.

"You don't ever need to be sorry. You've been through a lot. I don't want to rush you into anything," Torin reassured her as he turned to face her on his stool.

Placing both of his hands on her arms he pulled her to him in an embrace. *It is okay, we can wait as long as you need,* he told her in her mind, soothing her scattered thoughts.

I want you, please, Torin. She leaned up and kissed him tenderly.

Torin stood as he kissed Grace, his hands moving down to her hips, he turned her on the stool. As she wrapped her legs around his waist, he lifted her from the stool and carried her to the couch across the room. As he laid her back on the couch, Grace kept her legs wrapped tightly around his waist. As Torin smiled down at her she unhooked her ankles from behind his back and watched him take hold of the legs of her pants, pulling them off her.

She pulled her own shirt off over her head, not having put a bra or underwear on when she got up to answer the door, she lay naked on the couch in front of Torin as he looked down at her. His eyes trailed over her body. The wounds he could see from the Dorcha made him sigh, he wanted to wash it all away for her. As he pulled his own shirt off over his head, he tossed it to the floor.

Grace took him in, the toned muscles of his chest, the V shape at his hips that disappeared below the waistband of his sweatpants. She smiled a wicked smile at him. Climbing onto her knees on the couch, she leaned forward and pulled him free of his pants, then took him into her mouth. Swirling her tongue over the head of his cock as she reached up and took his balls in the palm of her hand. Torin tossed his head back, looking at the ceiling. The feel of her mouth on him making his need for her grow.

Grace swallowed every inch of his cock, pushing him into the back of her throat, her tongue trailing up his shaft as she eased back off him. The moan that slipped from Torin drove her forward, wanting to continue to please him. Looking up at him she smiled around him filling her mouth.

Tell me what you want, she prompted him in his mind.

"Mmm, my wee fairy. I want you bent over this couch on your knees with my cock inside you." She glared at him as he spoke, hating the term fairy. He chuckled at her, his hand cupping her chin, "Don't be so sassy. You like it," Torin said and winked at her.

Grace slipped her hand between her thighs, her fingers finding her clit and circling it. She rocked back and forth as she continued to suck Torin's cock. Wanting to find her own release as she pleased him. She didn't want anything between them at that moment. Not Beth or Rowan, their ghosts from the past had haunted them last night. She felt Torin tense as she thought of their names.

I'm sorry. It's me, it's just me. Just us, she reassured him.

Continuing her motion on her own clit as she sucked him hard into her mouth again. Torin looked down at her, an unspoken command in his eyes calling to her. The word leapt forward into the forefront of her mind.

Master.

Torin froze, his hand on Grace's head. He pulled her back from him. Knelt on the floor beside the couch and looked deep into her eyes. The memories he could see swirling in her mind at that moment struck him through the heart.

"No," he said and shook his head, a tear slipped from the corner of her eye, and he brushed it away with his thumb. She felt like she had let him down, she had made him angry with her and she didn't understand why.

"No, Grace. I'm not angry. But I am not your Master, you are not my slave. We are going to do this together as partners. A team." He pulled her face to his and kissed her on the forehead.

"A team?" she gasped. The idea of having him support her, him being by her side, caring for each other. It warmed her insides.

Torin nodded. "We are a team, Grace. Together we will get through this. No matter what it takes. Do not see me as above you." She nodded. She didn't know how to place what she was feeling.

She had this image in her mind of serving Rowan, of being at his beck and call. Giving in to his every demand. They hadn't been together long, but it was the only form of love she had known. She jerked at her own thoughts. It had not been love. It had been manipulation. Abuse, he had been using her. She needed to separate the truth of that from the lies she still had swirling in her mind.

"Hey, look at me," Torin said and brushed his thumb over her lower lip as she pouted. "We do not have to rush this. You need time. You need to heal." Leaning in, he kissed her gently.

Grace sighed as they kissed, the tension leaving her body. She didn't know what had been driving her to this moment. Why she felt so desperately that she needed to please him with her body. Torin pulled her into his lap as he settled onto the couch next to her.

"I'm not going to reject you, or this, or us because you feel like you've failed me somehow." Shifting her on his lap, he kissed her on the top of her head and continued, "I do not have expectations for you to be some woman kept in my bed at all times, here for me whenever I demand it. I want to know you. Learn who you truly are. To be with you as your partner in this life and the next."

Grace was dumbfounded, the kindness she heard in his

words, the truth of them that she felt. It was unlike anything she had experienced in her life. Left by her father and alone once her mother died, she had spent so many years alone, centuries. Torin wanted to be with her, wanted to know the real her. Her heart soared.

"What do you want to do today?" Torin asked her, as he rocked her in his lap.

The ghosts of their past had won out again. How long would they continue to interfere in their life?

"Can we head to Glasgow?" It wasn't that she didn't want to spend the day with Torin, but she was eager to get training with Quinn. They could spend time together on the way there.

"I'd rather you have Quinn sift you there. From Keep to Keep. The wards that are protecting you both from the Dorcha are strong. The journey there would leave us out in the open," he explained his decision to her, and she felt as if she had a choice. He wasn't telling her what to do.

Grace nodded. "I'll call her. See if we can start tomorrow then. Today can be for us." She made the decision to forgo her training with Quinn for one more day. Her time would be better spent with Torin anyway. Torin smiled, happy to have this time with Grace.

"Let's get back in bed, I'll bring you breakfast. We can veg all day." Grace smiled at his words. "I'll head down to the kitchen and see what Ma' and Olivia baked this morning."

"Mmm, sounds amazing. I'm going to take a shower." Grace stretched and stood. Torin patted her on the behind as she hurried away from him, sending a quick smile over her shoulder.

Torin headed through the Keep, seeing Cassidy and Seamus in the hall together he made his way toward them.

"Quinn said you had no luck with the Roneys and the Burren?" he asked his brother as he approached.

"No, Da', Dale, and Colin are coming up with a plan B. We are going to leave at nightfall." Torin nodded, as Seamus spoke.

He didn't want to leave Grace. But he knew if she stayed in the Keep then headed to Quinn tomorrow, she would be safe. It was still early. They would still have the day together as they had planned.

"I'll come," he told Seamus, "I want to be there when we find him." His desire for revenge was stronger than the one to stay here with Grace. Twisted with his emotions over Beth and revenge for her as it may be, he gave in to it, nonetheless.

Seamus nodded at him, understanding written on his face. He left the hall then, heading to the kitchen in search of food for them to hole up in his apartment all day together.

CHAPTER
FOURTEEN

GRACE STOOD under the scalding water of the shower, it stung the cuts on her back and arms. She needed it to wash away the memories with the blood. Needed to eliminate Rowan from her mind completely. Everything she did, every time she had a thought, something he had shown her, something he had done crept into her subconscious.

She was beginning to realize how deeply he had twisted her mind. How far he had slipped into her life and her heart and turned her into his slave. Every time she saw his face in her head, she heard the words he purred in her ears. *Master, bow before me*, she shook her head as she heard it now. Clear as if he were in the shower with her whispering it to her once more.

She was assaulted with the images of her on the ground, her arms stretched out above her head, bowing low to him. Her naked body was covered in blood as he looked down on her. The memory wasn't her own, she was seeing herself from his perspective. Suddenly fear streaked through her and she looked around the room. Making sure she was alone. There were no signs of anyone here with her. But she felt a presence. She could feel his hands on her arms, his claws trailing down her back.

A scream ripped through her. Torin burst into the bathroom, concern covering his face. He saw Grace in the shower, alone, her knees pulled up to her chest as she rocked back and forth on the floor. He pulled the shower door open and turned the water off, steam filled the air of the small room. Pulling a towel from the rack, he wrapped Grace in it and lifted her in his arms.

Taking her through to the bedroom he sat down on the bed with her in his lap. "Hey, talk to me. What's wrong? What happened?"

"Rowan, he was here. With me. It was so real." Torin shook his head as Grace spoke.

"It isn't possible. The wards protect you. He can't enter the Keep." Brushing his hand down the back of her head he rubbed her back.

"But I felt him," she said, but she wasn't trying to argue. She knew what she felt. Knew the truth of it. She could still feel the burn on her back from his claws. "He was here, my back…" she sniffed.

Torin shifted her in his arms, her back still had the same marks it had when he left her. Different stages of healing showed the passage of time as he had bled her again and again. There was nothing new marring her skin.

"You're safe, Grace. There is no one here." She sighed at his words.

Her mind was playing tricks on her. It wasn't that she needed him to believe her. She needed to find a way to regain control of her own mind. To be able to believe him that she was truly safe, and that Rowan had not been here.

"Torin, I need help. I need to erase him from my memory. I need the images of him gone. This was different. This was new." She struggled to find the words to explain what she was feeling. She needed to explain what she felt, what she saw.

Confusion filled her and she shut down, she turned inward to her mind trying to block out what she had just experienced.

"Don't do that," Torin said and turned her in his arms so he could see her face. "Don't block me out and turn away from me. We're a team, remember?"

"It isn't you I'm trying to block, it's the world, everything else," she said and sighed.

"Get dressed, I've got breakfast. We are going to veg." Torin wanted to reach her, but he didn't know how to do it. He needed to talk to Brody again.

Brody and Faith had been through this, but they had had a lifetime together beforehand to know one another. A lifetime of memories to use to block out the ones Faith wished to forget. He didn't have that with Grace. He decided instead to show her his life, to show her his past. The hundred years he had spent as a wolf. The things he had learned, the pain he had felt at losing Beth. All of it.

They lay in bed eating flaky pastry while he delved into his own mind and showed her who he was. His past, his present, his plans for their future. Grace did the same, she showed him the life she had lived with her mother. The time she had spent with her father, the help Seamus had provided her with when the Fae turned their back on her. She showed him all the things she had studied at Trinity, working in the libraries.

As the sun began to set, they felt at peace, both sat in the other's arms, watching the magic they had invoked in the air between them swirl above their heads. The room was filled with it, the magic of their bond, the love that was growing between them.

"I have to go," Torin said and moved over on the bed, his hand falling over Grace's hip. The relaxed contact between them felt so natural, so comfortable.

"Where?" She knew the answer already. He was going with his pack to the Burren to find Rowan. "Never mind," she said and heaved a heavy sigh. "I'll call Quinn and see if she can come get me tonight or in the morning."

"What's wrong?" Torin looked at Grace's face, watching it fall.

"I don't want you to go." It was the truth of how she felt, she didn't mean to guilt him at all but she didn't want him to go.

Grace wanted Torin to come with her to Glasgow like they had planned this morning. Even more now that they had spent the day together. She didn't want to be apart from him.

"I have to do this, Grace. For both of us to have peace of mind." She nodded as he spoke.

She could distract herself with Quinn and not think about the fact that they were separated. She tried not to think about her shower, the things she had felt. The fear that had gone through her mind. Knowing that Rowan was gone would help her. Torin was right about that. It would help them both to have the ghost from her past not trying to hunt her down in this life.

Rolling onto her side she turned her back to Torin, reaching behind her, taking hold of his hand she dropped it over her side. She wanted him to hold her for as long as he could.

"Wait until I'm asleep?" She wanted to have this moment with him. Wanted him to slip out after she was asleep. She didn't want to watch him go.

"Sleep, Grace," Torin whispered in her ear, kissing her cheek. Pulling her closer to his chest he held her in his arms until the sound of her breathing changed. Then he crept from the room and headed to find his brothers.

Grace woke, her body covered in a cold sweat. She could feel the presence in the room with her. Rolling onto her back she searched the shadows carefully.

"Hello?" she called to the empty room.

My sweet, Grace, he purred into her ear, she jerked, looking to the empty space in the bed next to her. *I've come for you, Grace. Come to me.*

Robotically she rose from the bed, swinging her legs over the side of it. She rose and crossed the room to the door. Her hand settled on the doorknob, and she looked down at it. Confusion over what she was doing filling her mind as she moved through the apartment. When she entered the hallway of the Keep it was silent. Everyone was asleep in their own beds, there was no one to stop her. No one to help her.

Torin! she cried out for him in her mind.

Master! Rowan's growl filled her mind.

"No!" she screamed.

Descending the stairs one step at a time, she tried to stop herself. Tried to lock her knees in place. The only effect it had is that she nearly fell down the stairs face first. He wasn't here. This wasn't real. He couldn't reach her in the Keep. She squeezed her eyes closed as her bare feet touched the cool stone of the great hall.

"Cassidy!" she screamed at the top of her lungs, tears falling down her cheeks. She knew her friend was the closest to her in the massive castle. If there was any hope of someone hearing her it was Cassidy. "Cassidy!" she screamed, her lungs burning with it, her throat sore.

"Grace?" she heard the voice call her. "Grace?" She couldn't turn to see who was calling her name. "Grace!"

Her hand was on the knob of the massive front door, the night air swept in as it creaked open.

"Grace!" Arms closed around her, and she fell backward. The spell was lifted, as she collided with the stone floor, her legs tangled with the woman who held her in her arms. "Dear heavens, what are you doing, dear?" It was Gwen, Torin's mother who held her in her arms as they lay on the floor in front of the door.

It swung open the rest of the way and there in the courtyard Grace could see the pair of red gleaming eyes. She screamed.

Bow! he ordered her. She shifted on the floor, her posture forced as she bowed to him. Her King, her Master. He had come for her.

Gwen stood, looking across the threshold. She saw the Dorcha. She had no fear, for she had encountered it time and time again in her centuries. She had held Faith in her arms on this very step as she watched the creature take shape in the shadows the night it had chased her home. She slammed the door, a gust of wind swept through the hall.

"Be gone ye' evil beast!" Gwen shouted the words. "Ye' are not welcome here! Go! Gone with you!" Gwen continued as she looked down at Grace's form on the floor at her feet.

Cassidy reached the top of the stairs at the far end of the hall, hearing the chaos. She made out the form of Gwen standing by the door, a dark shadow at her feet.

"Grace?" she asked as she came closer.

Kneeling next to her she placed her hand on her friend's back. She could see Grace's face was wet with tears.

"Torin," Grace sobbed.

"He isn't here." Gwen knelt on the opposite side of Grace, her hand placed on her back below Cassidy's.

"I can't move," Grace gasped, trying to shift her body from the position she was locked in on the floor, bowing. "Why can't I move?" Panic started to fill her.

Suddenly the door creaked, Gwen and Cassidy looked up. All three women could feel it, the presence of the Dorcha on the other side of the door. A roar ripped through the night, snarls and growls following. It clawed at the door, Grace knew this was it, he was going to take her again. The wards on the Keep were going to fail.

Silence fell over them. Grace felt her body relax. She regained control over her limbs. Rolling onto her back she looked up at Cassidy and Gwen. Breathing a sigh of relief. It was over, he was gone. She was safely in the Keep and the Dorcha was gone.

"Thank you, Gwen," she said and let the older woman wrap her in her arms. Cassidy rubbed her back gently.

"'Tis gone now. Though I fear if I'd not been here, you would be gone as well," Gwen said and sighed. She needed to speak to Declan. They needed to find a way to keep Grace safe here in the castle. This would not do, having the Dorcha on their lands was one thing, having it trying to take control of Grace and get her to leave the castle was dangerous.

"What the hell just happened?" Cassidy spoke up. She had come into the hall after hearing her name being called to see Gwen practically tackling Grace as she tried to leave the Keep.

"He was here, Rowan, the Dorcha," Grace turned to Cassidy, "He was in my head. I'm almost positive he was in my dreams. Then I could hear him, I lost control of my body. It was like when I was with him again. He had power over me, over my mind and body. This time he had power over my body, but I was aware of it. I could feel it was wrong, but I couldn't stop it. The wards around the Keep they're keeping him out. But not keeping me in."

"We can fix that," Cassidy said and smiled. "Seamus put up wards to keep me in, can't we do the same for Grace?" She turned to Gwen, thrilled that she had a solution.

"Aye, we can. But it will take time. I fear we may not have much of that before it returns. It knows the pack is not here. It has returned for Grace. It may be better to secret her away." Gwen knew she could put up the wards that they needed but it would take hours they may not have.

"Quinn, she is supposed to take me to Glasgow. I can call her now. I can leave," Grace offered the idea to the others.

"Aye, then we would have time to get the wards in place. But you would need to return, you cannot stay at the Roney Keep. If we put the wards up here to keep you in then you'll need to be on the correct side of them," Gwen thought it through. With Declan gone she was in charge, and she needed to make a decision. "Call Quinn. Go to the Roneys for now. Cassidy can help me put up the wards, we will let you know when it is safe to return."

Grace was sad with the decision, she wanted to stay in Glasgow with Quinn, she wanted to train. She didn't want to come back here, locked in the Keep with wards, waiting like a sitting duck for the Dorcha to return and lead her around like a puppet. She would be slammed against the wards, like a bug against a pane of glass again and again as the Dorcha tried to reach her.

"I'll call Quinn." She headed across the great hall, back up the stairs, to Torin's apartment for her phone. She would call Quinn and go to Glasgow, but she resolved to stay there and not return. She waited for the call to connect.

Quinn's sleepy voice broke through the silence. "Grace?"

"Hey, I need you to come get me. Gwen and Cassidy are here with me. The Dorcha is here on the O'Gannigan lands. Quinn…" Her voice broke, the memory of not having control over her own body filled her mind. "I'm not safe here. It's trying to get me to leave the Keep. I need your help."

"Okay, let me get things together here. I'll be there as soon as I can." Quinn ended the call.

Grace headed back down to the great hall to find Gwen and Cassidy. "Quinn is coming," she told the two women as she headed to the table in the hall where they sat. Taking a seat next to Gwen she was grateful when the older woman placed her hand over hers and squeezed it. Tears welled in her eyes.

"Are you all right?" Cassidy asked her, the concern on her face for her friend was obvious.

"I will be," Grace sniffed. Cassidy nodded.

"I'll make us some tea," Gwen offered, patting Grace's hand and rising from the table.

Cassidy and Grace sat in silence while Gwen went to make them tea. Both looked up when they felt the magic in the room.

Quinn had appeared in the great hall. "I let Abigail and Avalon know we are coming. Are you ready?" She rubbed her hand on Grace's back between her shoulder blades.

It wasn't lost on Grace that all their lives had been turned upside down and everyone was going through this because of her actions, her failed spell was the cause. She nodded at Quinn and stood. She was ready to head to the Roney Keep. Still set in her resolve that she would not return here. She was working on a plan of her own.

"I'll help Gwen with the wards. We will call you when it is safe to return," Cassidy said and nodded at them, and Grace slipped her hand into Quinn's.

In the blink of an eye, she stood in a nearly identical great hall. Abigail and Avalon Roney rushed towards her and Quinn.

"Sifting will be on our list. We should start simpler. But I want you to be able to get some of the big things out of the way," Quinn's reassurance filled Grace with hope.

She knew this was the right choice, happy that she had talked to Torin about it, and he supported her growing her powers. Hesitation filled her mind over how he would react when she told him she wasn't coming back until she had learned everything she needed from Quinn, but she was set on her decision. She needed to call him though, to let him know what had happened. Quinn approached the other two women in the hall and Grace decided it was now or never. Slipping her phone from her pocket she dialed Torin's number.

"Hey, why are you up?" he immediately started with questions. "Is everything okay? What happened?"

"Rowan..." Grace swallowed hard, his name sticking in her throat. "The Dorcha was here. Well, not here. But at the Keep. Quinn came and got me. I'm in Glasgow."

"Grace, are you okay? What happened?" As he demanded answers she could hear the voices of the others in the background, clearly tipped off by his voice that something was wrong.

It sounded like chaos, so many wolves together. All of them knew their mates were in danger and had been left behind in their respective homes unprotected. Now they were starting to get the phone calls. She heard Declan and Seamus both speaking, bits and pieces of it made it clear they were on calls of their own with Gwen and Cassidy.

"Grace?" She had been distracted listening to the melee, Torin's voice pulled her back to him.

"Yes, I'm here. I'm sorry. Yes, I'm okay," she breathed a heavy sigh. "He was there. He had control of my mind, my body. I almost left the Keep. Gwen said she thought it best if Quinn came and got me. So, he wouldn't know where to find me. She and Cassidy are going to put up wards so when I go back, I can't leave the Keep, same as how he can't get in."

"Aye, I'll come to you. Can Quinn come get me?" Grace glanced up at Quinn still talking to the other women.

"I'll ask her. But, Torin, I don't want to go back. I don't want to be caged in and slammed against that cage night after night. I want to stay with Quinn. I want to train and be able to protect myself." He was silent on the other end of the phone. She knew he didn't like the idea.

"I respect that. I know you want to be able to protect yourself, Grace. I don't agree, I need you where I know you'll be safe—"

"So have the Roneys put up wards here. But I'm not leaving. I'll see if Quinn will come get you. I have to go, Torin." She didn't give him the chance to respond and ended the call.

"I'm not going back." Grace cleared her throat as she approached the three other women.

"What's this, dear?" Abigail asked, a look of concern on her face.

"I want to train with Quinn. I don't want to go back to the O'Gannigan Keep as soon as they have the wards up. I deserve the chance to learn to defend myself." Grace's face fell as she took in the looks on the faces of the women standing around her.

She knew these were strong, powerful women who had been through centuries of struggles. She refused to let them cow her into something she didn't want to do.

"Aye, we could put up wards here just as easily as Gwen

can," Quinn offered, the only one obviously on her side. "I think it's fair."

"I need to speak to Colin about it," Abigail offered. Grace knew as the Alpha of the Roney pack he would have the final say and no doubt Torin was already filling him in.

Grace just nodded, a yawn escaping her, looking down at her phone in her hand she realized it was nearly dawn. She had awoken the whole of two households with her inability to keep Rowan out of her head. She needed to start there with Quinn. Needed to not only be able to hone her magic but to guard her mind from the Dorcha.

"Quinn? When can we get started?" She was eager, impatient even and sleep could wait.

"Aye? Now I suppose," Quinn said and turned to Abigail and Avalon, "do you two need us for anything right now?"

Both shook their heads and Grace took that as their cue to leave and be on about their training. Quinn guided her through the Keep to her apartment.

"Are you truly all right?" Quinn asked now that they were in the privacy of her apartment.

"Aye, I'm shaken up, I won't lie. But I am all right. Honestly, I'm more angry, than anything else." Grace was almost to the point of fuming. "I need you to teach me to protect my own mind. To block him out."

"It would be much easier if he had not previously been there. He knows your mind now, perhaps better than you do yourself. We will make a go of it though." Quinn sat on the couch and patted the spot next to her. "You need to turn inward, find the place where no one can reach you. Delve deep, it is there. You need to pinpoint it. It is where your magic is as well. So, starting here is not a bad steppingstone to have you tap into that."

Grace thought about Quinn's words. She thought she had reached that place in her mind in the past. But the time she spent with Rowan had taught her that she hadn't. The place she felt was her own, he had crept into with her. Closing her eyes, she pushed inward through her memories. She was able to clearly pick out those that did not belong to her, both the magic laced ones from Rowan and those that Torin had shared. As she floated downward through her subconscious she found it, a dark corner of her own mind she had never visited. Shifting on the couch, she changed her perception. Suddenly she was looking at a door with a gleam of light flowing out from the crack beneath it.

Reaching out, she placed her hand on the knob and waited a moment, steadying herself. As she pulled the door open the magic in the room behind the closed door burst through the opening and she felt it surge through her body. Her eyes flew open and when she looked down her fingertips glimmered.

"You found it!" Quinn gasped, pride filling her.

"Yes, now what do I do with it?" Grace was filled with excitement.

"We're going to tap in to it! But next time the Dorcha comes for you, this is your safe haven. You go to that place, and he will not be able to reach you." It seemed simple enough to Grace, it was a room. She could lock herself in and be safe. It made her feel safe for the first time in days.

"Okay, how do I tap in to it though?" Grace eyed Quinn, not understanding.

"The hard part is done. You found it. You already know how to use your magic. Now you have it in the palms of your hands. You can do the rest." Quinn smiled.

"That's it? That's all you're teaching me?" Grace was disappointed, she had expected so much more.

She had gone to her father and begged for help. Had it been this easy all along? She didn't know why she hadn't been able to figure this out on her own. Her face fell as she thought through what Quinn told her.

"You've got this, Grace. You are so much more powerful than you have been giving yourself credit for. You don't need me to show you anything else. Why don't you try something?" Quinn had confidence in her friend. She simply wished Grace felt it in herself.

"Like what?" Grace thought it through, she knew how to glamor things. Would this new access to her power make that more believable? She turned inward into her mind, making an attempt at glamor without snapping her fingers or thinking of a spell in her mind.

Quinn gasped, "Grace?" Her friend had disappeared before her eyes. She hadn't expected her to try sifting as her first step. Grace's laughter filled the room. "Ah, I thought you sifted!"

"Glamor!" Grace squealed. "But to be fair I already knew how to do this."

"Okay, then why not try something else. I'd really like some tea." Quinn watched as Grace reappeared before her.

"Tea?" Grace's brow knit together as she focused in on her mind.

At last, waving her hand and looking down at the puddle that appeared on the table before them.

"Oh shit!" Grace cried out as it dripped onto the carpet.

"Next time try a mug?" Quinn laughed.

"That makes sense, I was simply thinking of tea. Not a mug of it. This is going to take some serious thought, like I need to be precise." Grace sighed.

"Aye, but you did it. Try again." Quinn patted Grace's thigh, hoping to infuse her with some of the calm she felt.

Grace's eyes widened. "Will I be able to affect people's emotions, too?"

"No, that is not Fae magic." Quinn didn't go on. Grace knew better than to dig, if Quinn wasn't going to offer more information, then it would be pointless anyway. "Tea?" Quinn tried to get her back on track.

"Tea," she agreed. Waving her hand again, this time focusing on the more specific details of what she was trying to summon.

On the table before them appeared two small teacups, sitting on saucers and full of steaming tea.

"You got it. Now, how about some scones to go with breakfast?" Quinn knew she was pushing Grace, but she wanted to learn, and she wanted to learn fast.

"Blueberry?" Grace licked her lips. A plate of scones appeared in her lap. She nearly dropped them in surprise at how easy it had been to conjure them.

They sat and ate in silence. Grace played in her mind as she closed her eyes and chewed, sipping her tea every so often.

"Ready to sift?" Quinn asked.

"What if I end up in the middle of nowhere? I didn't ever imagine that would be possible for me." The panic in Grace's voice was evident.

"You won't. Just sift to the other side of the room. Don't try anything crazy, picture the space you want to be standing in your mind. Grab your magic in your hands and will it. Same way you willed the tea and scones. You have it in you." Quinn was encouraging, but Grace had her doubts.

Nevertheless, she closed her eyes, picturing the spot on the other side of the room where she hoped to end up. Digging deep she willed herself there. She felt the sifting, the magic of it that she was familiar with. When she opened her eyes, Quinn was seated on the couch in front of her grinning from ear to ear.

"I did it?" Grace looked down at her feet, the space around her, taking in her surroundings. "I did it!" she screamed, the words full of excitement. "Okay, what about sifting to people?"

"I think we should hold off on that, places you are familiar with are the easiest. A person could be anywhere, somewhere you've never been. It could land you in a dangerous situation." Quinn wanted her to learn, but she knew certain things would take time. "Want to try more glamor? Convince me we are somewhere else."

Grace scrunched her face, she had only ever attempted to glamor herself, not project it to another being. Pulling an image into her mind she looked around at the walls of the apartment. Then the furniture, slowly things began to take shape. Swaths of magic filled the living room. Opening her eyes, she was looking at the cave in Wicklow where she and Rowan had been together. Quinn was seated on the couch in the corner, looking at the bed Grace had been bound in.

"Where are we?" Quinn asked.

"Wicklow, with Rowan." Grace took it one step further. Focusing on herself, rather than making herself vanish from sight she painted her body with the memories of Rowan.

Quinn gasped, "Grace?"

"Aye?" It was still her voice, not Rowan's that fell from her lips. "Well, that ruins the illusion doesn't it?" She giggled.

Quinn guffawed at hearing her friend's voice coming from the man's mouth. "Yes, it does. But it's absolutely hilarious. Try again," she urged her to dig deeper into the glamor.

"Quinn?" Grace spoke again, hearing his voice, not her own this time and smiling.

"That's disconcerting," Quinn stood and approached Grace, "but you're doing it. I'm convinced."

Dropping the magic Grace looked around the room again. Quinn's apartment had returned to its perfectly manicured self.

"Ready for me to take you home?" Quinn was exhausted. She needed to rest and figured that Grace would rather be back with Torin.

"That's really all?" Grace felt more confident now, but still wasn't convinced that this was everything she needed to learn.

"The rest is just practice," Quinn reassured her. Grace nodded.

"Torin is on his way here. I need to call him and tell him I'm coming back to Kerry," she sighed.

"I can get him and Cian, stay here." Quinn vanished before her eyes.

Grace was jealous she wanted to be able to do it all now. She didn't want to practice, but she had learned her lesson the night she brought the Dorcha back by mistake. Magic was not to be played with. Quinn, Cian, and Torin reappeared in the apartment's living room. Torin closed the gap between Grace and himself and scooped her into his arms.

"Ready to go home?" he asked her, kissing her cheek.

"Aye," she said and yawned. The morning had been exhausting after a night that left her nerves frayed. She was ready to go home and get in bed with Torin.

Quinn silently placed her hand on Torin's arm and in the blink of an eye they were back in his bedroom.

"Call me if you need anything," Quinn told Grace as she sifted out and returned home.

CHAPTER
FIFTEEN

"TELL ME ABOUT IT?" Torin asked as he settled them onto the bed back in his apartment.

"Let me show you." Grace summoned forth the memories of the morning pushing them to Torin across their bond.

He smiled at her, pride over her coming into her own strength filling him. Grace would be a force to be reckoned with.

"Okay, but what about last night? What happened?" He was glad she had shared this with him, but he needed to know about the Dorcha and what had happened in the Keep that led her to flee in the wee hours of the morning.

Grace sighed, shame over her own weakness filled her heart. She didn't want to be so out of control ever again.

"It was awful." A tear slipped down her cheek, and she buried her face into Torin's chest. "It was like I was a marionette puppet on strings."

"The wards are up, Ma' and Cassidy had Faith and Olivia help. They finished them before we got back."

Grace knew Torin's words were meant to comfort her. In reality they made her feel like she was trapped in a cage. She snuggled into his body further, trying to draw from his warmth.

"I don't wish to be slammed against wards night after night when he returns," she said, making her feelings clear.

"What Quinn taught you will help you to protect yourself against him." Torin rubbed her back trying to reassure her. "Want to test it out?" he asked her, hoping his idea would give her some confidence.

"How?" Grace sat back and looked into Torin's eyes.

Block me. He spoke in her mind through their bond, sending her images of them together. Then the memories she had shared with him from her morning with Quinn. *Block me out, Grace.*

She dove into her mind, seeking out the door to the chamber she had within her. Torin continued to bombard her with images. Slowly she opened the chamber full of magic, then stepped in and slammed the door behind her. It was silent. Torin's voice was gone, the images were gone. She stood alone in the chamber surrounded by her magic. It was so peaceful.

"Let me in?" Torin coaxed her, brushing his knuckles down the side of her face.

Grace turned and swung the door back open. Torin stood on the other side of it in her mind. She watched as he took a step forward into the chamber, she held out her hand to him. Together they stood surrounded by her magic. In her mind he leaned in and kissed her. Their own magic burst into the space mixing with hers. She felt as if she were floating. Having him here in the deepest recesses of her mind with her was so perfect.

I love you, Grace, he told her as they continued to kiss.

She sighed into his mouth as he kissed her. Pulling a ball of magic into her hand she waved, and the chamber transformed. They no longer stood in an empty space surrounded by magic. Torin looked around and saw his own bedroom had appeared in Grace's mind. Gently he guided her backward toward the bed as he continued to kiss her. Grace lay back on the bed, holding her legs out to him so he could slip her pants down over her hips. Sitting back up, she helped him remove her shirt. Then watched as he undressed the rest of the way. Sitting on the edge of the bed in front of him naked, she looked up at his naked body and smiled.

It's just us in here, Grace told Torin. She couldn't feel anything between them except for love and magic. Their ghosts were gone.

Torin climbed over her body on the bed as she lay down on her back and wrapped her legs around his waist. As he slipped inside her pussy, the feeling of having her wrapped around him made him groan. The swirls of magic around them shifted, the blues, yellows, and greens, of their bond twisted in with the pinks and purples of Grace's inner magic.

It's beautiful, Torin told her, *you're beautiful.*

Slowly Torin rode Grace, sliding in and out of her heat again and again. Grace could feel herself climbing toward her climax. She wanted this so badly. Wanted to be with him at last. Torin rolled on the bed, taking Grace's hips in his hands and settling her on top of him. Grace took the lead, riding him, she ground her clit down on him as she buried him to the hilt in her pussy again and again.

Come for me, Grace. I want to watch you come for me. Torin coaxed her closer to the edge of her pleasure.

Grace tossed her head back, her hair falling down over her back. Torin ran his hands over her bare back, twisting one into her hair at the base of her neck. The other slipping around to take a breast into his hand. As he pinched and twisted her nipple between his fingers she cried out, bucking against him harder. Chasing the high she was feeling spread through her body.

I'm going to come, she screamed in her mind.

Look at me, I want to see the look in your eyes as you come all over my cock. Torin demanded it of her, twisting his hand in her hair he bent her down over himself. Looking right into her eyes as they glimmered with ecstasy.

Grace relaxed, the tingle moving up her legs reached her clit, and she came. Grinding herself onto Torin's cock as she felt her cum seep out between their bodies.

Fuck! he growled.

Torin could feel his balls tighten against his body. His cock swelled inside Grace. Both of them could feel it, as he pulsed inside her, jerking with each spurt of cum that filled Grace, he wrapped her in his arms and pulled her to his chest. Each heaved heavy breaths as they lay together on the bed. Their legs twisted together. Grace could feel Torin's heart pounding in his chest. At last they had connected, no regrets, no memories, no past had shoved its way between them. She glowed from the inside out, her skin alight with her magic as she twisted her fingers through the swirls of it in the air.

Come here, she purred in Torin's ear. Opening her eyes and looking around his bedroom.

Both here now, in reality, they lay in the bed fully clothed. Torin shifted Grace on the bed, he slowly undressed her. He had experienced her in his mind. It was time to lay their ghosts to rest and do the same in this life. Grace matched Torin's movements. Undressing him as he had done her. She slipped her naked body down on the bed next to his. Grinding her ass back against his cock.

"Mmm, Grace." Torin gripped the base of his cock and rubbed the head of it up and down her slit.

As he pushed forward into her. Grace arched her back. An arm wrapped around her body, his hand grasping her breast, and he held her tightly to his chest as he entered her from behind.

"Don't stop," she panted. The feelings she had experienced in her mind with him were so real they had her close to the edge already as he filled her.

Rolling her onto her stomach he pushed deeper into her pussy, riding her hard and fast, he needed to mark her, needed to claim his mate at last. Sliding his hand under her hip he found her clit and rubbed circles over the taut bud. Grace pushed her ass further back against him. She needed him deeper inside her. Needed more of his hands on her. His fingers continued to rub her clit as he took his other hand and pinched her nipple. The assault of sensations filled her with pleasure, and she cried out.

"Come for me, baby," he whispered in her ear. The stubble on his chin scratched her ear lobe as he spoke.

It was enough to push her over the edge, Grace moaned as she came, her climax shaking her body. Torin could feel her trembling beneath him. Slipping from her and bracing himself on his knees he tapped her on the hip. Grace rolled onto her back and Torin settled between her thighs, closing his mouth over her soaking pussy. Pushing his tongue inside her he could taste her cum, relishing the taste and scent of her. She tangled her fingers in his hair pushing his mouth further down on herself. Wriggling beneath him, she arched her back. Craving more of his mouth on her, she did all she could to encourage him. His tongue lapped at her, fingers filling her as he continued to devour her.

"Torin, please. I need to come, don't stop," she pleaded with him.

Mmm, never. Come for me. I want to feel you come all over my face, he purred in her mind.

"Fuck!" She gasped out the word as he reached up and smacked her breast then took her nipple in his fingers and twisted it. "Torin, I'm coming!" Grace cried.

Yes, come for me. He crooked his fingers inside her, rubbing her inner walls. Then pulled them out and replaced them with his tongue as she clamped down around him, he felt her coat his face and smiled into her pussy.

When he leaned back on his knees and looked up at her, Grace could see her cum coating his face and chin. She held her arms out to him, and he lay over her body again, kissing her gently. She could taste herself on his lips.

Slowly he slipped into her, she was soaked. "God, you're wet and ready for me," Torin sunk deep into her.

Bracing himself on his arms positioned on either side of her face he looked down into Grace's eyes as he fucked her hard and fast. She wrapped her legs around his waist, grinding herself onto him further.

Torin, she hesitated a minute, *choke me.*

His hand wrapped around her throat, and he pounded forward into her.

Take all of me, baby. I want to feel you come on my cock and milk me. The look in her eyes encouraged him. She liked it hard and rough.

Grace nodded at his command. Focusing on the feelings of pleasure coursing through her as he cut off the blood flow to her brain and bombarded her body with the sensations of having him fill her. Having her nipples pinched and pulled, he bent and closed his mouth over one of her breasts and she cried out, garbled as it was by his hand still on her throat. It was all she could take she squeezed her eyes closed, seeing stars, feeling the orgasm quake through her body. Torin thrived on it, the feel of her tensing around him as she came. He bucked hard inside her, filling her with hot streams of cum. As he pulled himself from her pussy, he coated her stomach with it.

Looking down at his mate, she was his at last. In their minds, in their hearts, in reality. They had overcome everything between them and now she was his.

CHAPTER
SIXTEEN

GRACE AND TORIN spent the rest of the day in bed. She conjured them lunch and dinner and they ate like kings. Joy filled her at how her abilities were growing and how much easier it was coming to her now. She sifted in and out of the rooms of his apartment, testing out her new skills. By the time night fell she was buzzing with excitement, but so exhausted she could hardly hold her eyes open.

"Get some sleep," Torin whispered into her ear.

Torin knew he needed to greet his father and brothers when they returned from the Burren so they could come up with a plan. Their trip there had been useless. By the time they arrived the Dorcha had already returned to Kerry, to Grace, and the Keep. They would be doing shifts, patrolling the Keep, tonight. They needed to search for signs of him. But they had discussed it before he left them with Quinn earlier in the day, and all then agreed that the Dorcha's desire for Grace's Fae blood would keep him here on O'Gannigan lands so he could try to get her out of the Keep again tonight.

Torin smiled at the thought, what he knew was that Grace had found a way to stop him in his tracks. Torin remained confident that tonight would be much different than last. As Grace slept he heard the noise of his brothers in the great hall beneath them. Creeping from the bedroom he headed through his apartment and down the stairs.

"How is she?" Seamus was the first to ask.

"Good, she spent half the day with Quinn. She has learned a lot and is catching on fast," Torin beamed. "I have little doubt she will block the Dorcha from entering her mind again."

"Aye, good to hear," Cormac said and smiled at Torin.

The four brothers settled into chairs around the table in the hall as Declan took his seat at the head of it.

"Dale and Colin have both returned home with their packs. We all need to protect our own lands right now until we find a way to track and eliminate the Dorcha," Declan told his sons.

"He will be back, he needs Grace. We will find him," Brody said with confidence.

"I'll take the first shift," Torin offered, he didn't want to be away from Grace all night. He would rather return to her in the night than wait until sunrise.

"I'll come with you," Seamus offered.

Torin and the others nodded. Brody and Cormac agreed they would take the second shift. As Torin and Seamus headed out of the Keep into the night Brody turned to his father and remaining brother.

"We need a plan. We are simply going to hunt him down and gut him?" Brody wanted clarification.

"Aye," Cormac nodded, "that's Torin's plan."

Brody sighed, "We don't think it will be more difficult than that? I can't help but feel we are missing something."

Declan rubbed his chin, unsure of the right answer. "We have tried every other spell in the book in years past. Banishment was the only thing that we could succeed at. We can expect that in this form we can kill him once and for all."

"Then why aren't we out in mass with the other packs searching for him so we can end this now?" Brody at last voiced his true concern.

Declan looked down the table at his sons. "Aye, let me see what I can do."

A scream tore through the Keep. All three men jumped to their feet.

"It's Grace," Cormac said.

"No, it's Faith!" Brody said as he took off up the stairs.

Grace rushed out into the hall, hearing Faith's screams from down the hall. She nearly collided with Brody as he reached the top of the stairs.

"I've got her," he told her as he rushed by.

Watching Brody disappear into his apartment the screams fell silent, and Grace returned to bed. Just as she was falling back asleep another scream tore through the night. This time as she entered the hall she nearly collided with Cormac.

"Olivia!" he called her name as he rushed past Grace in the hall.

She stood outside the door of the apartment this time, the realization of what was happening dawning on her. Grace took off down the stairs, she knew who was left. Cassidy's screams filled her ears as she burst into Seamus's apartment.

"Cassidy!" She rushed to the bedroom down the hall. "Cassidy!" She tried to wake her friend as she thrashed in the bed. "Wake up," she rubbed her back as she watched the tears stream down Cassidy's face. "Wake up, I'm here, you're safe. You're in the Keep. Wake up." Cassidy opened her eyes and looked up at Grace.

"Seamus!" Cassidy cried out her husband's name. "Seamus is dead."

"No, he isn't," Grace reassured her.

"I saw it, I saw the Dorcha kill him." Cassidy fell into Grace's arms and wept.

"No Cassidy, the Dorcha is here. He has been messing with all your dreams, he is…" she trailed off as it occurred to her exactly what Rowan was doing. "He is using you all to get to me. Fuck!"

Cassidy looked up at Grace. "What?"

"I blocked him out and he is using you three to get to me." Grace was lost in thought again.

"Hey, talk to me," Cassidy was the one comforting her friend now. "What's going on?"

"I need to go to him. I can't let him do this to you all. He wants me." Grace made the decision.

"No, Grace you can't!" Cassidy's words fell on deaf ears.

Right before her eyes Grace vanished. Cassidy stood and took off for the door of the bedroom. Grace was nowhere to be seen.

In the great hall Declan was the only one remaining at the table. Grace appeared at the door of the Keep.

"Gods in heaven, lass. What are ye' up to?" Declan stood when Grace didn't turn to him.

Grace heard him, she hadn't expected any one to be here and she had to work fast. She waved her hand and a knife appeared in it. She knew this was dangerous, knew it could backfire, but it was the only way she knew how to terminate the wards that as she looked down, she could see the blue and red shimmer of them carved into the back of the door. She realized she didn't know which of them she needed to eliminate, didn't know which ones were keeping her in and which ones were keeping the Dorcha out.

"Grace!" Cassidy reached the top of the stairs and came into the hall, seeing Declan she screamed, "Stop her!"

Grace took a guess, pulling the knife across the palm of her hand she saw the blood well up from the cut she dropped the knife and pressed her palm to the blue rune directly in front of her. The magic stuttered, it twisted black and blue before her eyes until at last the glow died. She swung open the door and stepped out onto the front steps of the Keep. The cold winter's night air kissed her skin, and she looked around. There were no signs of anyone here. She spun as she heard footsteps behind her.

Her eyes locked on Cassidy's. "Grace, please, you don't have to do this!" Cassidy pleaded with her as Declan raced towards her.

Closing her eyes, she pictured the tunnel in her mind, the Burren. The last place she had been with Rowan. She could see the memory clearly in her mind's eye. She focused in on herself. Took a deep breath and just as she felt Declan's hands close around the tops of her arms she was gone. When she opened her eyes, she was standing in the dark tunnel, the scent of Rowan filled her nose.

"Rowan!" she screamed his name at the top of her lungs. She wasn't sure if he would hear her.

He was more than likely in Kerry in the woods surrounding the Keep since he had been tormenting Faith, Olivia, and Cassidy. She should have thought of that. She wasted her time coming here. She needed to go to him. But this was something she hadn't tried. Sifting from Kerry to the Burren was the farthest she had managed. She didn't know if she could actually find a person. Quinn had warned her against it.

"Fuck," she said, then stomped her foot. "Okay," she said and took a deep breath in through her nose and blew it out through her mouth. "Where are you, Rowan?"

She tried to picture him, not him in a specific place. Not either of the caves, simply the man himself.

Diving into the room in her mind she gathered all her magic into her fists and pushed with her whole mind. "Rowan," she called to him.

"My saving Grace," he purred in her ear.

Opening her eyes, she saw him before she felt him. His arms closed around her and pulled her to his chest.

A snarl filled the air and when she turned, she saw it, the silhouette of a wolf in the field behind her. She recognized him instantly, another wolf appeared next to him from out of the woods. They took off towards her. She had two options. She could distract him and let the wolves do what they were determined to do. Or she could do it herself, she focused on her mind again. A knife appeared in her hand. As she drove it into Rowan's side he roared. The knife sunk into his side under his ribs. She could feel blood trickle down her hand.

Frantically she looked back at the wolves, they were almost to her. So close she could hear their footfalls hitting the grass with each step they took. She had done it, they were so near and Rowan had been injured. At last this would all be over.

Suddenly she felt it. She blinked while looking around, she was in the Burren again. Rowan had her pinned back against a wall. His other hand pressed to his side as blood seeped between his fingers.

"How?" she gasped.

"Mmm, you aren't the only Fae in the land for me to steal from. She was delicious," he licked his lips.

"Quinn?" Grace screamed, panic filling her.

She saw something in Rowan's eyes, he pushed the memory into her mind. It wasn't Quinn, a blonde Fae lay on the ground at his feet. Her heart in his hand. Grace gasped as she saw it play out, tears stung her eyes. Her heart ached for the fallen woman. She didn't know who she was, how it happened, how he had found her. But it was done, and in the past, she needed to focus on her plan. She didn't block him from her mind, she shattered the memory that he was feeding her and pushed one of her own into his mind.

The two of them together in the dolmen the first night she summoned him. Rowan purred in her ear, "Grace."

She could feel the magic crackle around them when she glanced down at his side it gleamed purple. His hand came away from his knife wound clean. She cursed in her mind. She had hoped this would be easy, hoped she could distract him until he lost enough blood. Gritting her teeth, she dove into her mind again. She needed to change tactics. Rowan wrapped his arms around her, startling her out of her mind.

"Let's not play these games with each other, Grace, we must

make haste." He wanted to get her to the chamber where they would be safe.

She nodded. Her head swam. She had been so confident in her abilities. What she hadn't expected was for Rowan to have any Fae magic left. He was right, it was no use. They could both fill the other's mind with illusions and shatter them just as easily. She would have to wait it out. If enough time passed, she would have the upper hand and she didn't need to give that away just yet.

"Let's go," she said and smiled up at him. Reaching up on her tiptoes and kissing him.

He wrapped her in his arms, pressing his mouth hard against hers. His tongue pushed between her teeth, and she fought back the snarl she wanted to let out at him for being so rough, for taking what was not his to take. Instead, she rubbed herself against him, desperate for him to believe her ruse. Hands roamed down over his back, slipping forward into the waistband of his pants.

"No," he barked at her, "not here. We are out in the open. Come." Breaking away from her he held out his hand and as Grace settled hers into it her skin crawled.

She would have to be convincing, and she knew in order to do so it meant she was going to do things she would regret. Things Torin may never forgive her for. She steadied her breath. She could leave now. Go back to the Keep and let the wolves do their jobs. Or she could find her resolve, follow through with what she had put in motion, and end this on her own. As she followed Rowan down the corridor, she wondered how long it would take for the Fae magic he had, to fade? How long would she have to lock herself away with this monster and convince it she wanted him?

She couldn't return to the Keep and let him return night after night, haunting the innocent women there, whose only crime was knowing her. She knew that was not an option. Her only choice was to move forward. To continue on the path she had started down and hope for the best.

THEY WALKED FOR WHAT FELT LIKE HOURS. AT LAST GRACE SAW THE runes covering the stone walls on each side of the corridor and she knew they were close. She yawned dramatically as they entered a cavern and the space opened up around them. She knew she could choose to furnish the room herself, but the more she had him use his stolen Fae magic the sooner he would deplete his supply.

Standing back, she watched as Rowan waved a hand and the lavish furniture appeared before her. A massive bed filled the center of the room, the look in his eyes told her what he wanted. What his expectation of her was now that she returned to him.

"I'm starving, and so tired." She rubbed her eyes and headed for a table sitting on the opposite side of the space from the bed.

She knew she was a terrible actor. It would take more than a yawn or two to get out of what Rowan clearly had planned for them. Not to mention her failed attempt to kill him was no doubt going to come back to torture her as soon as he was settled.

As she sat down, a spread of food appeared before her. "Thank you, Master," she cooed. Knowing this would please him.

She knew then what her misstep was. She should never have walked into the room and straight to the table. The words filled her mind as the memories washed over her. Grace rose from her chair. Turning, she fell to her knees and bowed before him. It was too little, too late. As she fell to her knees her eyes made contact with Rowan's and the anger that covered his face was evident. She didn't move, her arms stretched above her head.

Her breathing slow and steady, she tried not to let the fear coursing through her show.

Rowan circled Grace, a predator surveying his prey. She knew she had angered him. But she couldn't allow him to feed on her blood or the waiting game would never end. She wondered if the bond he had created between them went both ways, the way hers and Torin's did. Keeping all this to herself, she had her thoughts locked away in the room in her mind so he couldn't skim them. Torin had told her that her thoughts were loud, she needed them to be silent. Creeping out of the room in her mind, she looked around, surveying to see if Rowan was here with her. Determining he was not, she resurfaced and remained still on the ground at his feet.

"My sweet, Grace," he spoke to her, not in her mind and she breathed slow and steady. "Come here." She could see him in her peripheral vision, settling onto the bed. Calling her to him.

She crawled then, on her hands and knees like an animal. Like his slave, the way he craved. Settling into a kneeling position next to the bed she waited for her next command. He rose and crossed behind her, his claws extending from his fingers. He dragged them down her back, Grace screamed. The pain shot through her. Claws met bone as he dug them into her shoulder blades.

She felt her vision dancing, she was close to passing out and fought to remain conscious. When his hand turned soft on the bare skin of her arms, she flinched. Rowan growled low in her ear, "Do not fear me."

She shook her head side to side. "Please, Master," she begged, her voice soft. She didn't wish to be punished further.

"Please what?" His tongue grazed up the side of her neck. She knew what he was going to do, images of him doing this in the past filled her mind.

He bombarded her with memories of her giving him this gift graciously. Taking a chance she attempted to push back at Rowan. She wanted to test it out and see if the connection went both ways. As she brushed against the edges of his mind, she felt them give way, she fed it to him then. The glamor of her own making.

She pushed the image of Rowan sinking his fangs into the side of her neck into his mind, as she ground her body back against him. Mixing the truth with it she pushed her body backward. If she could make him believe the lie, she could survive this. Gasping in the moment as he closed his mouth over her neck in her mind. She was sure to do the same here in life.

"Master," she purred as she showed him images of him feeding on her. She couldn't be sure if he was buying it. If the glamor was holding up under his scrutiny.

Deep laughter filled her mind, and she froze, realizing now it would be trial by fire. Her strength was nothing compared to his, thousands of years old, he had told her. She had only been discovering herself for a mere twelve hours.

"Sweet Grace, you thought to distract me from the fact that you tried to kill me?" Rowan's voice was sweet, and it made her believe for a moment that it wouldn't be that bad.

"Master," she croaked.

The glamor she was projecting into his mind shattered, and she stood in the room with Rowan once more. Tears slipped down her cheeks at the reality of how stupid she had been to think she was capable of doing this. Goosebumps spread over her skin as he trailed his tongue up the side of her neck and she felt his fangs graze her.

"Mmm, I missed you." Waving his hand as he spoke, she was naked before him. Her hands bound to her waist with a thick rope that wrapped around her hips.

Fingers trailed down her arms and she trembled beneath his touch. Praying in her mind to whatever Gods might be listening that this end. She knew that Torin and the others knew where to find her. They would be on their way here. Reality of it was that it would take them hours, if not a full day, to reach her.

"Rowan," she whispered, hoping to tap into his softer side. The version of him she met on their first night together.

"Grace?" he purred in her ear, enjoying teasing her in this way.

"Please, Master. I'll behave. I had to. The wolves were there. If I didn't, they would have come after us both," she tried to reason with him.

"Don't lie to me," he said as he trailed his tongue down the side of her neck again.

Taking the head of his cock in his hand he slid it up and down her slit. "Mmm, ready for me, sweet Grace?"

Pushing on the center of her back he bent her over the bed, exposing her to him. "Master, please. Let me show you how grateful I am that you took me away from that place." Tears stung her eyes as she spoke. "I left the Keep. I came to find you. I did not expect them to be there in the woods."

Rowan positioned himself next to the bed at Grace's mouth. She parted her lips and took him in it. If she could sate his needs, maybe, she thought, she could catch him off guard with her glamor again. Hands twisted in her hair holding her still while he used her mouth for his own needs. He didn't buy it for a second, he knew she wished him dead and fancied herself more powerful than him when she tried to lie to him with the images she fed him.

Grace pushed inward into her own mind, searching for the door she had under lock and key. She found it quickly, the path leading her there more familiar now. Just as Rowan dove into her mind she slammed the door closed behind her. Eyes unseeing, she looked around the empty room she stood in. Magic sparkling at her fingertips and over her skin. The memories of her time with Torin here hung heavy in the air.

Torin! She tried to call him. *Please, what have I done!*

Silence was the only response. She was alone. The Dorcha had hold of her mind and body and she cowered in the corner in the back of her mind watching it all happen. Grace peeked out from under the proverbial blankets she had buried her head under. Watching the Dorcha use her, feed on her, and leave her lifeless body on the bed.

He would leave to feed. She knew this. Perhaps then she could escape. She hadn't played her full hand and shown him all she was capable of. She simply had to get out of the room and beyond the runes and she could sift back to Torin. The only issue she had is that while she was able to function in her mind her body would not behave. She had been bled nearly dry, her limbs felt heavy, like lead weights lay on her arms and legs. Summoning the magic in the room around her into herself, she gathered it. Now she must watch and wait.

Rowan climbed onto the bed next to her, pulling her bound body against his. He begrudgingly lay down next to Grace. This form was tired and had to rest, it enraged him that he must leave himself in this vulnerable state. At last, he slept. Grace put all of her focus into exiting the room in her mind with all of her magic inside her. She refused to leave a speck of it behind, she needed it now. As she opened her eye a slit she looked at Rowan's sleeping form next to her. Her body still felt weak, she was exhausted, and she could hardly hold her eyes open.

Using every ounce of energy, she had she focused on her magic and tried to will the bindings around her body to vanish. It was no use. She was too drained. She couldn't summon enough strength to do anything for herself. Grace's eyes fluttered closed, she retreated in her mind to the chamber where she felt safe, she had no desire to be out in the open and vulnerable to what Rowan had in store once he woke.

CHAPTER
SEVENTEEN

TORIN STOOD in the great hall, his family surrounding him. Cassidy sobbed into Seamus's shoulder.

"I'm sorry I couldn't stop her," Cassidy sniffed.

"This is not your fault," Torin said as he looked down at the map he was using to scry for Grace.

It was pointless, he had been trying for hours with no luck. He knew what it meant, it led him right to her, the absence of an answer was answer enough.

"They're in the Burren, we must go." He turned to his father, waiting for the final decision to be made.

"Aye, I'll alert Dale and Colin to our plan," Declan said, pulled his phone from his pocket and headed to his study to make the calls he needed to make.

"I just don't understand," Faith spoke up.

"She said she wouldn't let us be tormented by it and she needed to put an end to this," Cassidy sobbed.

"She thinks she can take him down on her own. Before he sifted them out, she stabbed him," Torin said, thinking through what he had witnessed in the woods. Fear for Grace and what the Dorcha was doing to her at this moment coursed through him. "We have to hurry. I'm calling Quinn, she can get me into the Burren faster."

Stepping out of the circle of his brothers, he pulled his phone from his pocket and dialed Quinn's number.

"Torin?" She sounded exhausted. He knew they had been putting her through a lot in her condition and he felt awful about it. But he needed to save Grace.

"Can you come here and get me to the Burren?" He didn't explain further.

"What's happened?" Quinn's voice broke.

"Grace left the Keep to find him on her own. We can't track her. They have to be in the Burren again. I need to get there as quickly as possible." He still didn't give her more than minimal facts.

"She isn't strong enough to do this. What the hell was she thinking!" Quinn's frustration was apparent, then she said, "Let me talk to Cian, I'm on the way." The call ended and Torin turned to Seamus who stood by his side.

"I'm coming with you," Seamus told him. Torin simply nodded, he was grateful to have his brother by his side through all of this.

Declan reentered the hall and announced, "The others are on their way." Nearly bumping into Quinn as she appeared in his path, he stepped back looking at her, and then to Torin he raised an eyebrow.

"Shay and I are going now. We need to search the Burren for where they're hiding out. We can find them while you are on the way and have a location to give you when you arrive." Torin stared his father down while waiting for his response, he didn't need his permission, but out of respect he waited for him to acknowledge his plan.

Declan nodded slightly. Torin looked at Quinn, heavy circles under her eyes told him she wasn't getting enough sleep. He felt guilty for dragging her into this again and again.

"Thank you," he whispered to her as he held his hand out for her.

Seamus took his place on Quinn's opposite side and the three of them were gone.

Looking around the tunnel they stood in, after Quinn dropped them off and left, Seamus and Torin decided it best to split up and search. They could cover more ground that way. There were miles of tunnels beneath the ground here and while Torin was confident they would find them. It could realistically take them days.

Shifting, Torin pushed his nose to the ground and began to search for Grace's scent. At least then he would have a lead to follow. He wasn't picking up on anything, he would have to search every path and room he came across until hopefully he would pick up a sign of her. Hours dragged by as he circled back around to paths he passed again and again. Exhaustion began to take him over and he was starting to feel hopeless.

Grace? He called to her through their bond, hoping that maybe he was close enough to her that she could hear him.

Silence, was all he heard, both in his mind and around him. It was useless, he wasn't even sure if he were standing next to the room she was in if the magic being used to keep him from tracking her would stop him from being able to reach her across their bond as well. Exhaustion began to take over Torin's body, his eyes burned, and muscles ached. He hoped Seamus was having better luck than he was, but the silence he heard stretched on for miles. No signs of a single howl to indicate his brother had found anything.

***

GRACE WOKE WITH A JOLT, ANGER FOR HAVING FALLEN ASLEEP filled her. She eased herself onto her side on the bed. Looking around cautiously. She was alone.

"Rowan?" she called quietly, she wasn't sure how near he was and wanted to ensure she was actually alone.

No response left her feeling brave enough to try to use her

magic again. She focused on her bindings, and as if they had never been there, they vanished. She stretched on the bed, glad to be free of the ropes that pinched and rubbed her skin raw. With the wave of a hand, she clothed herself and stood from the bed. Heading to the door that led to the passageway they had arrived in she made to exit the chamber.

It felt like she slammed into a brick wall, falling backwards onto her ass she hissed. Before she even tried to stand, she summoned everything she had and tried to sift out. The magic crackled and hissed around her, falling to the floor at her feet lifelessly. She was trapped, he had put up wards to keep her in. Grace stood and examined the runes carved into the doorway. This was not ward magic, she was unfamiliar with runes. She could try the same she had at the O'Gannigan Keep, but they were carved into the stone, and covered the walls, not just the doorway. She would have to paint the walls with her blood to break the spell and that seemed like a horrible idea. She turned, looking around for something she could use. Someplace she could hide.

There was nothing, she wasn't sure when Rowan would return, and she needed to come up with a plan. Her previous attempt to get into his head had failed, but if she could use glamor maybe she could buy herself some time. She moved to the far corner of the chamber and looked over it as if it were a blank canvas.

The day she had changed Quinn's apartment into the cave she had been with Rowan in and changed herself was all she could think of. She channeled that power now. Strokes of magic morphed the room. Her body lay bound on the bed once more and she stood invisible in the corner. Now, all that was left to do was wait for him to return. She wrapped her hand tightly around the hilt of the knife she had conjured in her hand. Time passed as she waited, she wasn't sure how long she had been here alone or how long it would be until he returned. She eventually sat, pulling her knees to her chest and waited, eyes trained on the door.

Grace? She flinched as she heard her name called in her mind. It was barely a whisper, but it was Torin, that much was clear.

She couldn't be distracted right now, couldn't let the glamor go. She was straining to keep it up for this long as it was and wondered if it was useless. It could be hours still before Rowan returned.

Torin, she whispered back to him at last. But there was no response. She had waited too long.

She knew what it meant, though. Knew he was here searching for her. She heaved a sigh of relief. She wouldn't have to do this alone. Another thought occurred to her, if he got here before Rowan, they could wait for him together.

Torin! she hissed in her mind, her excitement getting the better of her.

Grace! he responded this time and she nearly jumped up. Her glamor she had on the room and herself flickered.

Squeezing her eyes closed she took a steady breath, she needed to keep it together.

Where are you? he asked her, she could hear the desperation in his tone.

I'm in a chamber. I'm trapped, there are runes carved into the walls I can't leave. Rowan isn't here. She didn't want to bombard him with too much information.

What the hell were you thinking? Torin scolded her and she winced.

She knew he was there when she sifted into the opening in the woods, he had seen her, just as she had seen him. He was so close to reaching her when Rowan had sifted them out. She had injured him, and Torin was so near. Tears pricked her eyes as she thought about it, how foolish she had been.

We can't talk about that right now. How close are you? She was eager for him to get here before the Dorcha returned.

I don't know, there could be stone between us still. I've been searching for hours, Grace. I can't find you. The defeat in his voice scared her.

Torin, please. A tear slipped down her cheek.

I'm trying, Grace. Don't give up. I'm here. I will find you, Torin swore it to her. He looked around the corridor he was standing in. It was a dead end.

There was no sign of a chamber that Grace could be in here. He would have to backtrack again.

Grace, I love you. It will be okay. I have to go. This is a dead end. But I'm coming, just hold on. Her mind went silent, and she was alone again.

Looking over at the glamor she was throwing in the bed she saw her own naked body lying there. She took her time thinking through what she would do once Rowan returned. What would she do if he saw through the glamor the moment he walked in? So many thoughts rushed through her mind. She tried to quiet them, she needed to stay calm and remain focused. Turning inward for a moment she sought the room in her mind where she could be in peace. She didn't close the door as she entered and let her magic flow through her, she sat and watched through the open doorway and waited. Meditating, as she did. She needed to remain vigilant.

JUST AS GRACE feared she was dozing off she heard footsteps. Panic filled her and her hands and legs tingled from being in the same position for so long. She slowly stood watching the doorway of the chamber. Waiting, holding her breath, she tried to steady her nerves.

A shadow crossed over the threshold, and she tensed. The crackle of magic filled her ears, and she craned her neck trying to see what was happening.

Grace! Torin's voice filled her mind.

Torin! She nearly ran to him as she saw the figure of the wolf take shape in the doorway.

I can't get in. He stood in the corridor on the other side of the door.

Fuck, I can't get out. She wanted to weep.

She was so tired of this, she didn't know how long she had been waiting, but if Torin was here now maybe they had a chance. A dark feeling crept over her, and she knew instantly what it meant.

Torin, he is here. Her voice was shaky in his mind.

Torin spun in the corridor. A bear stood behind him on its hind legs. Crouching low he prepared to lunge forward at him.

Snarls echoed off the stone walls, coming from both beasts. Grace could hear the sounds of the fight but couldn't see beyond the door and didn't want to give away her position.

Torin lunged at Rowan, his jaws clamping down on his throat. He had mere seconds before the bear's massive paw splayed down his side. Claws tearing into his skin. Yelping he fell to the ground, as he stood, ready to fight he watched the Dorcha shift and dash down the corridor into the chamber at the end of it. Standing in the doorway he smiled, his eyes gleaming.

"Mmm, wolf," he said as he continued to look down at Torin. "Welcome, feel free to watch."

Torin knew he couldn't enter the chamber and Grace couldn't exit it. His eyes went wide as he watched the Dorcha turn to Grace's bound body on the bed. He didn't want to see this, couldn't watch what was about to happen to his mate. Rage filled him, he snarled and growled. Banging against the magical barrier in the doorway again and again.

"Mmm, my sweet Grace," Rowan purred to her as he approached the bed.

She wasn't sure how long she could convince him with the glamor. Once he reached the bed and tried to grab her, he would know it wasn't real. She thought quickly, trying to gather together her wits and come up with an idea.

Torin, leave, when I say hide. She knew what she had to do. Hopefully he would listen to her.

Slowly, silently in her bare feet she crept around the room behind Rowan toward the door.

One more time, try to get through. Now! Torin listened to Grace's words and slammed his body against the magic barrier.

He had expected it to give way to him, it didn't, instead he watched in astonishment as the form of a wolf appeared in the room in front of him. He ducked back down the hall, out of sight. It took him a moment to realize what she was doing. But he couldn't blow her chance at this, he tucked himself against the stone wall and looked on the best he could from his position.

Grace hunched low on her paws, she had to convince him. As a growl slipped through her lips she snarled, baring her teeth. Rowan spun, his eyes wide, taking in the sight of the wolf in the room with him. He knew it wasn't possible, how had the Druid done it?

He shifted from man to bear once more, approaching Grace as she continued to growl at him. She hadn't thought this through, she couldn't fight like a wolf. She didn't know the first thing about this form, and she wasn't even positive the glamor would hold if Rowan tried to harm her. The realization she had was if she didn't put an end to this she was going to be stuck here with him feeding on her forever. She needed to keep him from gaining any more of her Fae magic. Torin and the others were closing in and Rowan couldn't sift out of here.

If she put an end to this now, they would be able to end him. Everyone would be safe and the Dorcha dead, no longer simply banished, lying in wait to return. Dropping her glamor she stepped toward the bear, the knife she had conjured earlier still in her hand. She was resolved that this would end now, one of two ways, but one of them was going to have to die. Exhausted from trying to play games with magic and glamor, she knew what she had to do.

"Rowan," she took a step toward him, the knife hidden behind her back.

Torin's ears perked up as he watched the scene unfold before him. Dread filled his stomach as light glinted off the knife in Grace's hands.

"I'm done, I refuse to bow to you again," she growled at him through gritted teeth.

"Grace, don't be foolish. You know who is truly your Master, your King. You had the chance to be my Queen. Do not throw it all away over that mongrel," he spat the words at her looking behind her at Torin who stood in the doorway. "There is nowhere for you to go," he stepped toward her, "bow!"

She felt the command reverberate through her body, her knees buckled, and she fell to the floor, but she kept her spine straight and refused to give in to him any further.

Shakily, she stood once more. "Fuck you!" she spat at him.

Rowan's laughter filled the room. "I fully intend to. While your little pup watches. For an eternity if I must. You belong to me, bitch." Driving forward into Grace's mind he bombarded her with one command after another. Images of her bowing on the floor at his feet. She clenched her jaw and slammed herself away in the room in her mind where he could not reach her. Watching as Rowan's eyes went wide, she took yet another step toward him.

"You can't control me any longer!" she screamed the words at him. She realized she was trying to convince herself of the truth, not just him.

"Fine, we will do this the hard way," Rowan waved his hand.

Grace smiled at him, nothing happened. She stood firm where she was, unaffected by his attempt to cow her with magic.

"This will go one of two ways," she cooed at him, "but only one of us is going to leave this room alive." She meant it with her whole heart, she would do what she must.

The decision was made in an instant, Rowan lunged at her, and she knew she couldn't overpower him in a fight. She must do what she could to end this.

"Grace!" Rowan and Torin both screamed her name as she pulled the blade from behind her back and sunk it into her own chest.

Blood coated her lips as she coughed and yelled, "Fuck you, Rowan!" She knew as soon as he left the chamber, Torin, and the packs, would end him.

She couldn't allow him to use her to gain any further

strength. She collapsed to the ground and focused on her magic. She vanished before their eyes. Rowan stood staring down at the spot on the ground where Grace had just been. He raged, roaring, it bounced off the walls around him. Torin went mad slamming his body against the barrier that separated him from Grace. Rowan frantically looked around the room for her, but he couldn't find her. He needed to find her, to stop this. Grace smiled up at the ceiling. She gasped, her chest hurt, and her arms were going numb. She focused all her energy on the magic she had left and keeping herself hidden with her glamor.

"You son of a bitch! I'll rip your fucking throat out!" Torin screamed at Rowan.

"Try me, pup," Rowan said, shifted, and burst through the door into the corridor. His body colliding with Torin's.

Torin barely had time to shift, but he managed to just in time. Snarls ripped through the hall, followed by howls. They were here, Grace could hear them. She relaxed her body, dropping the glamor she was shielding herself with. As she rolled onto her side, she could see the melee in the passage on the other side of the door.

She stumbled to her feet and made her way toward the door. Looking out on the wolves as they attacked the bear, they took turns attacking until at last he collapsed onto the ground. The packs dog-piled on top of him, ripping him to pieces. It was done, the Dorcha was dead. She crumpled to her knees in the doorway. Resting her head against the magic barrier that locked her in.

Torin shifted, turning to the doorway. He saw Grace, the bloodstain on her shirt broke his heart. Pressing his hands to the barrier between them he wished with everything he had that he could hold her in his arms.

Grace, please. Don't give up. He pushed his thoughts to her across their bond. *We will get you out in time.*

The blood dripping from the knife wound in her chest fell to the stone ground, seeping into the cracks of the runes carved into the floor.

I love you, Torin. Tears slipped down her cheeks as she told him this. *I will always love you. Do not ever forget that.*

Closing her eyes, she floated through her mind to the room in her head where they had spent an incredible might together.

Torin? she called to him as she looked around the room filled with magic.

He appeared in the doorway, his arms wrapped around her, and she gasped.

I'm never letting you go, Grace. He pressed a kiss to her lips as she went limp in his arms.

Grace fell forward into Torin's arms. Shock filled him. He looked down at the puddle of her blood soaking into the runes on the floor where he knelt.

"Somebody get Quinn!" he called to the pack of men behind him. It would take them hours to find their way out of the Burren. He didn't have that kind of time.

No one moved, Grace's lifeless body lay in his arms as he turned and looked into the faces of his brothers, his father, and the members of the McTavish and Roney clans.

"Someone do something!" He fell forward onto his knees as he clutched Grace to his chest.

Dale stepped forward through the crowd of men in the hall. He had an idea, a spell from his past, but he didn't know if it was too late. The look in his eyes gave Torin little hope as he reached out for Grace. Torin lay her in Dale's arms, closing his eyes, he prayed to the Gods to intervene. As Dale spoke the ancient Gaelic words of the Druid spell, magic filled the air around them. Everyone watched and prayed, when the magic dissipated, and Grace's body remained the same, Dale shook his head.

"I'm sorry," he whispered to Torin as he lay Grace's body on the ground between them.

Torin collapsed next to her, for the second time in his life he looked down at the face of the woman he loved and prepared to say goodbye. Closing his eyes, he pictured her in his mind, the room she had shown him in her head.

He called to her there, *Grace, please. Come back to me.* He pleaded as he looked around.

The wisps of pink and purple magic were fading in the room, but they were still here. She was still here. He could feel her in the magic around him.

You can fix this, Grace, he told her. He knew it was possible. She simply had to find it in herself to heal. Fae magic had done far more with far less.

A thought occurred to him. It was his last hope. He pulled his phone from his pocket and dialed Quinn.

"We need you now!" He rushed out the words. "I need to get her to the dolmen in Kerry."

That was where this had all started, where Grace had tapped into the ancient fairy mound beneath the circle of standing stones. She had harnessed the magic there and used it for her spell. The veins of the earth ran deep with the Fae magic. It was why the Druids had chosen that place centuries later to erect their dolmen.

Come on my wee fairy. I know you're here, He called to her as he waited for Quinn.

Don't call me that. Torin smiled at the soft disgruntled voice that filled his mind.

Listen to me, I need you to hang on. Torin reached for her in his mind. *Don't let go.*

Quinn's voice broke into his mind, "Torin?" He felt her hand settle onto his shoulder and he scooped Grace into his arms.

Suddenly, he knelt in the middle of the circle of standing stones. Quinn knelt before him. She settled her hands onto Grace's chest, in an attempt to infuse her with some of her own magic. Torin settled her onto the grass, magic summoned up out of the ground by Quinn surrounded them.

"The rest is up to her," Quinn told him.

She looked down over the two of them, sadness filling her eyes. Torin nodded, he was grateful she had gotten them here and done what she could. Watching as she blinked out of his vision, he turned his eyes back to Grace.

Come on my wee fairy. He pushed himself into the room in her mind. Grace sat cross-legged in the center of the floor. Her eyes closed. *You have to do this.*

I don't know how. She opened her eyes and looked up at him.

Try, he insisted, *please Grace. Try for me.* Watching as the swirls of magic in the room disappeared into Grace's body.

She focused on it, gathering it all into her heart. She could feel the added strength that Quinn had infused her with. The extra magic that was seeping into her body from the ground beneath her. Pulling all her energy into her heart she held tightly onto it. Beyond that she didn't know what to do. Had no idea how to actually heal herself with it now that she had it gathered inside her.

Torin knelt in front of her in her mind. Pressing his hand to her chest over her heart. An idea occurred to her then, leaning forward she kissed him and as their magic filled the space around them she gathered it into her as well. Then in one swift motion she pushed it all from her and into Torin, his hands on her chest glowed with the magic.

His eyes flew open, and he was looking down at Grace laying on the grass in the circle of standing stones. His hands gleamed with the magic she had pushed into him. Just as he had done in her mind, he pressed them to the wound on her chest. The magic flowed from Grace's mind into his hands and then back into her body. She gasped and opened her eyes, looking up at Torin she could see the moon haloing his head, the stars in the sky above them gleamed.

"You did it, you wee fairy," Torin said and kissed her hungrily.

"Don't call me that," she grumbled against his lips. He cut off her words with another kiss.

We did it, she told him, *the Dorcha is dead.*

Wrapping her arms around Torin as he kissed her, she focused in her mind on the image of his apartment and sifted them there. She hadn't ever taken anyone with her before and she worried she would make a mistake. As she opened her eyes, she saw it had worked. They lay wrapped in each other's arms still, on his bed.

Torin broke their kiss and looked down at her, his hands cupping the sides of her face. "See wee fairy. We're sifting people now?"

"Aye," she said with pride, letting the fairy comment slide.

Leaning up she kissed him then, slipping her tongue between his lips she tangled it with his. She could feel the magic in the air between them and couldn't imagine life without it. Waving her hand, she made both of their clothes disappear and giggled when Torin's eyes went wide as they continued to kiss.

Grace ground herself onto Torin's cock as he pushed himself between her legs. Torin could feel the heat of Grace's pussy press against him. He wanted her badly, but as he looked down over her body, he saw the dried blood on her skin and the newly closed wound on her chest.

Sitting back on his heels he looked down at her. "Why don't we get cleaned up first?"

Grace took in the sight of herself and nodded her agreement. Torin stood, lifting her into his arms and carried her to the bathroom. As the shower warmed, he peppered her skin with kisses, worshiping her with his hands.

"I'm never letting you out of my sight again," he whispered against her belly between planting kisses on her hips.

"It's going to be a long eternity with you hovering over me nonstop," Grace said and rolled her eyes.

"Perhaps you should have thought of that before you ran off to play hero on your own," he scolded her.

Torin's words were soft, but the truth of the anger he felt at the decisions she had made, was evident in them.

"I'm sorry," Grace said and trailed her hands down Torin's bare arms as he stood before her.

He didn't respond, instead he reached around behind her and opened the shower door, they stepped inside together. Both standing under the spray of the hot water and letting it rinse away the grime and blood from what had transpired. Grace looked down at Torin's side, the puckered pink claw marks on his skin from where Rowan's claws had torn him open matched the mark on her chest. Both had healed but would remain scars for the rest of their lives. Her fingertips skimmed over the marks. She felt guilty, if she had not acted so rashly then Torin would not have had to come searching for her in the Burren.

Mere minutes were all he and Seamus had needed, and they would have taken Rowan down in the clearing here on the O'Gannigan lands. But she had sifted to Rowan and thrown a wrench in their entire plan. No, she shook her head at her own thoughts. Rowan would have sifted out with or without her appearance at that moment.

"Would you stop?" Torin asked and kissed her on the forehead. "All of this is for nothing. It won't change what happened. You can't go back now. Stop thinking so loudly."

Grace winced, she hadn't realized he was in her head listening to everything she was trying to rationalize. "I'm sorry," she said and meant it. Not just for being so engrossed in her own thoughts, but for her actions that had led them to all that had transpired.

"Hush," Torin said and kissed her, then turned her in his arms.

Slowly he washed her hair and body, soothing her aches and pains. Careful of her fresh wounds, he washed away all the blood from her skin. Grace turned to Torin and did the same, tenderly she brushed the washcloth over the scars on his side. When he reached around her and turned off the water, each grabbed a towel and dried themselves in silence. It was deafening. Grace feared Torin was angry with her, Torin feared she was slipping away from him.

Making their way back to the bedroom they stood and looked at each other, their ghosts were back. Standing between them once more. Perhaps they took on different forms this time, but they had returned, nonetheless. Grace sighed and settled onto the edge of the bed, as she lay her head back on the pillow and crossed her hands over her stomach she stared up at the ceiling. Torin lay next to her, draping his arm across her.

Grace? he called to her quietly.

Closing her eyes, she met him in her mind, he stood there surrounded by magic with his arms held out to her.

It's just us in here, he whispered in her ear as she let him hold her tightly to his chest.

Grace nodded, taking in the scent of him and burying her face in his shoulder. Torin rubbed her back gently, kissing her on the top of her head. Grace opened her eyes, back in the bed with Torin holding her. Rolling onto her side she tucked her body against his and listened to his steady breathing. Exhaustion started to take them both over as they relaxed and let the comfort of one another soothe them. Grace fell asleep at last, her dreams showing her all of the things she had done leading to this moment in Torin's arms. She dreamt of the night of Valentine's Day, the month she had spent with Rowan.

Waking up here in Torin's bed with Quinn and Cassidy by her side. The moment she and Torin first kissed, her puppet-like movements as she crept through the Keep as the Dorcha controlled her body. Her decision to leave, all of it played out in her mind. Torin lay next to her, not trying to intrude, but he watched it like a movie on a screen. All her emotions were so close to the surface, he understood her fears, her goals, the love she felt for him. A tear slipped down Grace's cheek, and he brushed it away with a kiss.

I'm right here. Always, he whispered to her as she slept.

Grace smiled softly, a small smile in her dream. It was all

right in her world. Everything that had gone wrong was fixed. There was so much that had gone right. In the end her spell had worked and brought her to her mate. The packs had at last eliminated the Dorcha and would be free of him for any future generations that might come. They would be free, free of the ghosts of the past, free of fear and doubt. None of it mattered as long as they had each other.

CHAPTER
NINETEEN

GRACE WOKE the next morning with Torin's arm still draped over her. Rolling onto her other side so she could face him she kissed his cheek. Slowly she sat up, swinging a leg over him she straddled his hips. Torin's hands settled onto her hips, and he cracked his eyes open, smiling up at her.

"Good morning my wee fairy," he said and winked.

His morning erection was pinned between them as Grace wiggled on top of him, grinding her pussy over him as she rocked her hips back and forth. Her slick pussy rubbed up and down his shaft as she ground herself down on him.

"Mmm, Grace," Torin called to her as he gripped her hips more tightly and pushed her harder down against himself.

Grace arched her back pushing her breasts out. Torin closed his mouth over her nipple, grazing his teeth over it. The warmth of his mouth on her, made her moan as he swirled his tongue over her.

"Fuck," she whispered the word. "I need you, Torin. Please." Her moans filled the room as he continued to lap at her breasts.

Sitting up, he wrapped his arms around her waist and lifted her from him. Positioning her on her knees on the bed he ran the head of his cock up and down her slit, then pushed forward into her.

"We can play just the tip," he teased her.

Grace tried to force herself backward onto him, but Torin quickly took hold of her hips and pinned her in place. Keeping just the head of his cock inside her as he stilled his motion.

"Torin," Grace whined at him shaking her ass.

"Yes, wee fairy?" he purred in her ear, slipping ever so slightly further into her as he leaned forward.

Looking back over her shoulder at him she scowled as she used her glamor to make wings appear on her back. Torin's laughter filled the room, and she wrinkled her nose at him. She could be a tease too. She sifted herself out of his grasp. Positioning her body on the bed next to him as he looked down at her wide eyed, her fingers on her clit. Grace moaned as she ran her other hand up her body to her nipple. "Two can play this game, Torin," she said and winked. Pleasuring herself as he continued to kneel next to her.

"Hmm, Grace. You want to play games?" Falling forward over her body he tickled her sides and she squealed.

"Please, no! I can't breathe! Don't tickle me!" she gasped.

Torin rolled her onto her stomach as she tried to twist away from his grasp. He pulled his hand back and smacked her square on the ass. Grace cried out, pushing her rump into the air for him.

"Again?" he asked, she nodded in response. "Mmm, dirty girl," he said and smirked, striking her on the ass again as she wiggled it for him.

"Yes," Grace hissed out her pleasure.

Torin took his time, alternating soft pats with hard smacks on her ass. Her pale skin turned bright pink as he bent and kissed her. It felt hot to the touch. Sliding his fingers up her slit she was soaked and ready for him. One digit slipped into her core, and she moaned.

"Please, Torin, fuck me," she whimpered.

Her arms were shaking from holding herself up and she was giving in to the feeling spreading over her as he used both his hands on her pussy. Fingers sliding in and out of her as well as circling her clit.

"Come for me, Grace. Come all over my fingers, maybe then I'll let you come on my cock." Frustration at his words filled her. She wanted him now. She didn't want to wait and be teased any longer.

Patting her hip, he coaxed her onto her back, and buried his face between her thighs. His mouth closed over her clit, and he pushed his fingers deep inside her. He nipped at her, running his tongue in circles over the bundle of nerves as she bucked against his mouth. When he bent his fingers and found the perfect spot inside her he stroked her, and she came undone beneath him. Grace came hard, it was wild, sparks flew behind her eyelids as she rode Torin's hand. The pleasure of so much teasing up to this moment had her panting for more.

Torin took his free hand and stroked himself up and down the length of his shaft in his fist. He wanted to be buried inside her, wanted to feel her throb around him as she came for him again. He lifted her legs, spreading them as he pushed himself inside her soaking center. Grace cried out, gasping at the fullness of having him in her pussy at last. When his pelvis pressed against hers and he was fully buried in her heat he stilled. Grace glared up at him, impatience filling her.

"Angry, wee fairy, aren't we?" He winked at her as he slipped from inside her, immediately pushing back in.

The feel of her walls tightening down around him as he pushed in and out of her made him moan, he tensed, focusing on keeping his composure.

"I want to watch you come all over me," he whispered to her as he slid his fingers down the inside of her thigh to her clit.

The motion of him inside her mixed with that of his fingers on her clit brought her right to the edge of her orgasm. Grace chased it headfirst and dove off the cliff into the pleasure as it washed over her. Torin looked down, watching as she came all over his cock. Pulling out of her pussy he motioned for her. Grace rolled, crawling to him on the bed.

"Suck your cum off my cock," he told her, and she smiled, nodding to him.

Closing her mouth around the head of his cock she ran her tongue in a circle over it. Tasting his precum and her own cum mixed together fill her mouth. Using one hand she cupped his balls, twisting them in her palm.

"Mmm, Grace," Torin said as he gripped the back of her head and pushed her down his length. Shoving himself into the back of her throat.

She took all of him, swallowing him as he fucked her mouth. Looking up at him she watched as he tossed his head back, pleased that she was giving him exactly what he wanted. As Torin released her, she slid him from her mouth, her tongue trailing up the underside of his shaft as she did. Her hand gripped the base of him, and she squeezed him, her hand following her mouth up and down his shaft as she sucked him.

"Fuck, Grace. Stop," he said, as he twisted his fingers in her hair and pulled her from him. "You're going to make me come. I don't want to waste it. I want to come buried inside your tight pussy."

She nodded, knowing it had worked, and she would get what she so desired at last. Shifting in the bed she positioned herself in front of Torin and he drove forward into her, smacking her ass once more as he did.

"Mmm," she arched her back giving him better access to her. "Fuck me," she growled at him.

Torin bent and growled in her ear, low under his breath, "Always, just like this. Hard and deep, take all of me. Come all over my cock as I fill you with my cum."

His words were her undoing, she ground herself back on his cock and when he smacked her ass again, she bucked as her orgasm took over. The feeling of heat moved over her body from her core, and she cried out. Torin gripped her hips, pulling her back on him harder. Pumping into her as he found his own release, he filled her pussy with it. Marking her once again as his mate.

They both fell forward onto the bed and Torin wrapped his arms around Grace pulling her tightly against his chest.

I love you, he told her in her mind. *Forever and always.*

I love you. She smiled as he kissed her shoulder.

EPILOGUE

ONE YEAR *Later*

GRACE SAT ACROSS FROM QUINN, A BABBLING BABY ON HER LAP. The pair of women taking turns conjuring toys and glamor for Quinn's infant as they spoke.

"When you live as long as we do, as long as we have, it is true that time heals all wounds, but time is relative to everyone. Some of us need more of it than others," Quinn told Grace.

"I get that," she said and sighed. Thinking about her original question and the meaning of Torin's love for Beth.

The past year had proven to her that their ghosts were not truly gone, and she wondered if they would ever be able to be together without them rearing their ugly heads between them.

"Think about how much you're still haunted by the things you did with Rowan," Quinn said, treading lightly. "Torin blames himself for Beth's death. You blame yourself for bringing the Dorcha back. You both need to face what your true responsibility was in those matters in order to let them go. If you ever want to be able to truly let them go."

"Aye, you're right." Grace knew her real motive behind being here and discussing this was her jealousy of Beth. Her fear that she wouldn't be able to live up to the memory of Torin's first love. It hurt her heart to admit this, she knew she needed to speak to Torin about it and not Quinn. "I should probably go home and talk to Torin."

"Aye, that is the most logical thing for you to do." Quinn reached out to take the baby from Grace's lap. "Remember he loves you. You are his mate, and he has committed to an eternity with you. Don't let the past ruin that."

"I know." Grace handed over the baby and focused on her magic, sifting herself home to Torin.

As she sat on the edge of their bed he rolled over and smiled up at her. Grace had left in the wee hours of the morning. Torin had been calling out to Beth in his sleep and it hurt her heart so badly that she fled their bed and ran to Quinn.

"Where have you been?" Torin asked and yawned.

"With Quinn, the baby is getting so big. It makes me happy to be able to be a part of her life, to be able to teach her, with Quinn, about herself and her magic from a young age." Grace wished she had had that for herself.

"What's the real reason you left before dawn?" Torin sat up on the bed, eyeing Grace.

"You were dreaming of Beth again," she told him the truth, the silence between them was so loud Grace nearly screamed.

"Grace, I'm sorry—"

"No, please don't be. I don't want you to be sorry. You don't need to be sorry. I understand. I truly do," she took a breath, "you blame yourself for Beth's death and—"

"Grace." She could tell by the look on his face that she misstepped. Torin was fuming, she gaped at him. She didn't know what to say and he didn't go on.

Both sat staring at the other as long moments ticked on between them.

I love you, Grace. I do not want this between us. But what it comes down to isn't that I blame myself, it is who I blame.

Grace nodded as Torin spoke in her mind, she gathered the

meaning of his words and when he rose from the bed and left the room, she watched his back. She knew he was going to seek out his father. They were the two who needed to clear the air between them after hundreds of years with this gulf between them. Laying back on the bed she searched her own mind for the answers on who she needed to forgive in order to get past what had happened with Rowan. She knew the truth, it was herself, but she simply wasn't ready.

TORIN ENTERED HIS FATHER'S STUDY, DECLAN SAT BEHIND HIS DESK, a book in his hands. "We need to speak," Torin told him as he took a seat across from him.

"I'd say it is about time." Declan nodded as he set down his book. Torin bristled.

He wasn't going to pretend that he was the only one who had been avoiding this conversation for so many years.

"Da'…" He wasn't sure where to start.

"Son, I was wrong. I was so incredibly wrong from the moment I ordered Shay to kill Beth, my actions following that, and for so many years. I can see that now. I can see the harm I did you. The poor innocent woman whose life I snuffed out, and for what? In the name of secrecy?" Torin's mouth fell open as Declan continued to speak, "I have been waiting for so long to tell you. I knew it would fall on deaf ears, until you came to me ready to hear what I had to say it was no use. I'm sorry." Torin bristled again.

Thinking that his father's evaluation of the situation was unjust, taking a moment before he spoke, he realized, though, that it was the truth. If Declan had tried to tell him this before now, he would have thought him full of shite and simply lying to win him over. His actions when Grace first arrived here, and all that he did to help save her. It proved to him that his father's words were in fact the truth. He had changed.

"Da', I'm sorry I left for so long, that I was too hardheaded to hear what you had to say sooner." His heart softened to his father.

"No, I wasn't ready myself, for many years. We need not dwell on the past any longer. Can we move forward, together?" Torin hoped they could, he nodded at his father's request. "How is Grace these days?"

The two had not spoken since need required them to a year ago, and for centuries before that the silence between them had only grown. Declan's concern for his wife now made Torin's heart open further to his father.

"She is still blaming herself for the Dorcha's return," he said and hung his head. He knew his words to be true, but it was something that even he and Grace did not speak of.

"No one is worse for the wear, she is safe. We are all still here. She need not continue to punish herself. Mistakes happen." Declan smiled softly at Torin as he looked up at him.

"Aye, I have told her so many times. She simply cannot let go of the guilt," he said and sighed.

"And how many centuries has it taken you to let go of yours, to come here and blame the person responsible rather than yourself?" Declan's point was clear.

Grace would continue to blame herself until she found a way to place the blame where it was truly owed. On Rowan, the Dorcha. The beast was the only one to blame for what had happened last year. She may have summoned the magic, but she was not attempting to summon him, he hijacked her spell and used it for his own needs.

"How do I help her?" Torin pled with his father, hoping he would have an answer to provide.

"Time, it will take time. A year is but the blink of an eye for us. You know this. So does she. Give her the time she needs to work through it. Be there for her when she needs you to be, and together, in the end it will all come to right." Declan's wise words had Torin nodding.

"Thank you." He rose from the chair, just as Declan did the same.

His father stepped out from behind his desk, walking around and taking him into an embrace. They stayed like that for a long moment. Torin tried to remember the last time his father had hugged him. It was hundreds of years ago. It felt right, to have put this to rest between them after so long.

TORIN ENTERED THE APARTMENT TO FIND GRACE SITTING CROSS-legged on the couch. He went to her, sitting next to her and wrapping his arm around her shoulders. Grace lay her head on his shoulder and listened to the steady beat of his heart.

"All is well?" she asked, not wanting to pry too much into what had happened between him and his father. But still wanting to know.

"Aye, all is well. We spoke. He apologized. Told me he was wrong for what he had done, and sorry for the loss of Beth." Torin went silent then, as he pictured the face of the woman he once loved in his mind, he steadied himself. It was time to let her go, to let the past remain in the past. "My ghosts are behind me, behind us. I love you, Grace. I will for an eternity and there is nothing that will come between us again." He swore it to her.

"My ghosts still haunt me, and I fear they will for a lifetime," she said and sighed.

"Aye, perhaps. But we have many lifetimes to live together. If a lifetime is what it takes, then in the next we will forget and move forward. I am here no matter what. I do not blame you. No one blames you. You need to stop blaming yourself. You did not summon the Dorcha, you summoned me, and he hijacked your spell and brought himself forward. You are not to blame." The rational words he spoke made sense to her. But her brain was not rational in the least. "Can I show you something?"

Grace nodded, she closed her eyes, knowing what he meant.

He wanted to show her something through their bond. She saw herself standing in the circle of standing stones at the dolmen. She had seen this before, or part of it rather. As the scene unfolded in her mind she saw him in the woods, the magic drawing him to her. The magic drawing her to look up at him, for an instant she did look up at him. She did see him, but before she had time to process that it was him Rowan was there.

He burst through the trees behind Torin, taking him over and rushing forward past him. It was all that Grace had seen in her mind. But from Torin's vantage point she could see the truth. She hadn't summoned Rowan, he had in fact taken advantage of the gap in the magic between her and Torin to insert himself.

Searching her own mind for her version of the memory she found it and pulled it forward. She had never noticed the magic around the edges of it before. This memory had been altered, but she didn't remember him doing it. The Dorcha must have affected this memory the moment it was forming in her mind, so long before he even made contact with her. She pushed her magic into it, shattering his that still remained woven through the strands of the truth.

She saw it then, Torin. He stood as a wolf on the edge of the circle. Their eyes met and, in that instant, she knew he was her mate. She could feel the magic, see it even. Gasping she opened her eyes and turned to face him. Tears slipped down her cheeks.

"I didn't summon him?" she cried.

"No, ye' did not, lass. Your spell worked. It didn't fail and bring back the Dorcha. You summoned your mate," Torin said and brushed the tears from her cheeks. Kissing her softly as he did.

"Thank you," she whispered to him. "Thank you for helping me see the truth."

Torin laid her back on the couch, his body covering her. He didn't bother to make an effort to remove their clothes. He knew Grace would take care of it. As if the thought had summoned her magic forth, they were both suddenly naked. She smiled up at him, lifting her hips off the couch and grinding herself over his cock as she did.

"Mmm, my wee fairy," he teased her. Kissing her on the tip of her nose.

"I'm not—" Torin cut Grace's words off with a kiss on her lips. Slipping his tongue into her mouth, through parted lips.

Hush, wee fairy, he told her in her mind.

Grace giggled, she didn't mind the teasing as much anymore and now she had little thought for anything other than Torin filling her with his cock. He slipped inside her and she arched her back moaning. Taking all of him in.

Torin slid his fingers over her clit slowly, bringing her body to life beneath his touch. Closing his mouth over one of her nipples and taking it between his teeth, he sucked her breast into his mouth. His hot tongue circled over her nipple, and she cried out.

"Yes! Torin!" Panting out slow steady breaths as he continued his assault on her breasts with his mouth. Moving his fingers over her clit slowly and filling her again and again.

"Come for me, Grace, I want to feel you come around my cock." His words were muffled by her breast still in his mouth. Grace giggled at him as he spoke. But nodded her head, following his command and focusing fully on the pleasure he was giving her.

Lifting her hips off the couch beneath her again she pushed her hips forward, tightening her inner walls down around him as he slipped in and out of her again and again.

"I'm going to come," she gasped.

"Good!" Torin laughed. "Come on my wee fairy." He winked at her.

Grace saw stars in her vision, the magic of their bond was filling the air around them and she let go of the slim control she had over her body. She came, hard, bucking beneath Torin's body. Torin drove home into her, as deeply as he could. He sought his own release. Grace trailed her fingers down his back, digging her nails into his shoulders.

"Mmm," he purred in her ear, "I'm going to fill your pussy with my cum."

"Yes," she was close to another orgasm. Chasing it down she ground her clit over Torin's pelvis as he fucked her.

"Come with me, Grace," Torin commanded her as his balls tightened and he felt himself swelling inside her.

They reached their climax together, Grace could feel Torin twitch inside her pussy, filling her with his cum as hers gushed out around him onto her thighs. Both collapsed onto the couch, panting, trying to catch their breath. Torin peppered Grace's neck and chest with kisses. Looking down at the scar on her chest from the blade she had driven into herself. His kissed the scar, hoping to brush away the memories from his mind. It seemed like each time they eliminated one ghost between them there was another that would appear.

Time would heal all wounds, just as their physical wounds had healed and they spent time focusing on healing their emotional wounds. These would heal as well. Today they each managed to leave something behind. He had let go of Beth and Grace had let go of Rowan and her guilt over his reemerging into this world. Time would march on, they would face it together, hand in hand. Fated mates for an eternity.

HER FATED MATE SERIES MAP

O'GANNIGAN

RONEY

MCTAVISH

Donegal

Mayo
Leitrim

Monaghan

Roscommon
Cavan

Longford

Galway
Westmeath
Meath

Offaly
Kildare
Dublin

Clare
Laois
Wicklow

Limerick
Tipperary
Carlow

Kilkenny
Wexford

Kerry
Waterford

Cork

Ireland

1498

DALE MATES WITH HOPE

DECLAN MATES WITH GWENDOLYN

COLIN MATES WITH ABIGAIL

1722

RORY MATES WITH SASHA

BRODY MATES WITH FAITH

FALLON MATES WITH AVALON

1723

CORMAC MATES WITH OLIVIA

CIAN MATES WITH QUINN

1725

LIAM MATES WITH CLARA

2023

SEAMUS MATES WITH CASSIDY

2024

SULLIVAN MATES WITH REESE

TORIN MATES WITH GRACE

CALLUM MATES WITH ROSE

EMMY LOU HAYES

Emmy Lou Hayes is a married mother of three. Originally from Ohio, she has lived the majority of her life in Maryland. While attending college she worked at a local sandwich shop, where she met her husband. When not working or at home in Southern Maryland, they enjoy spending time traveling the country in their RV with their children and two dogs. Emmy Lou works full time in the Medical field, but her passion is writing and sharing that writing with others. With an affinity for erotica and BDSM, Emmy Lou hopes to keep her readers coming back for more again and again.

Visit her website here:
http://emmylouhayes.com/

Don't miss these exciting titles by Emmy Lou Hayes and Blushing Books!

Marked Series
Branded
Scarred
Healed

Her Unexpected Mate Series
The Alpha's Melody
Second Chance Summer
For the Love of Sam
A Shift in Ciara

Broken Rae of Light

His Submissive Series
The Release
The Capture

Her Fated Mate Series
Finding Faith
Craving Olivia
Preying on Cassidy
Saving Grace

BLUSHING BOOKS
NEWSLETTER

Please join the Blushing Books newsletter
to receive updates & special promotional offers.
You can also join by using your mobile phone:
Just text BLUSHING to 22828.

BLUSHING BOOKS

Blushing Books is one of the oldest eBook publishers on the web. We've been running websites that publish spanking and BDSM related romance and erotica since 1999, and we have been selling eBooks since 2003. We hope you'll check out our hundreds of offerings at http://www.blushingbooks.com.